THE GUNSMITH

#51

DESERT HELL

Other Books
By
J.R. Roberts

Macklin's Women
The Chinese Gunmen
The Woman Hunt
The Guns of Abilene
Three Guns for Glory
Leadtown
The Longhorn War
Quanah's Revenge
Heavyweight Gun
New Orleans Fire
One-Handed Gun
The Canadian Payroll
Draw to an Inside Death
Dead Man's Hand
Bandit Gold
Buckskins and Six-Guns
Silver War
High Noon at Lancaster
Bandido Blood
The Dodge City Gang
Sasquatch Hunt
Bullets and Ballots
The Riverboat Gang
Killer Grizzly
North of the Border
Eagle's Gap

Chinatown Hell
The Panhandle Search
Wildcat Roundup
The Ponderosa War
Trouble Rides a Fast Horse
Dynamite Justice
The Posse
Night of the Gila
The Bounty Women
Black Pearl Saloon
Gundown in Paradise
King of the Border
The El Paso Salt War
The Ten Pines Killer
Hell with a Pistol
Wyoming Cattle Kill
The Golden Horseman
The Scarlet Gun
Navaho Devil
Wild Bill's Ghost
The Miner's Showdown
Archer's Revenge
Showdown in Raton
When Legends Meet
Desert Hell
The Diamond Gun

For more exciting
E-Books, Audiobooks and MP3 downloads visit us at
www.speakingvolumes.us

THE GUNSMITH

#51

DESERT HELL

J.R. ROBERTS

SPEAKING VOLUMES, LLC
NAPLES, FLORIDA
2014

THE GUNSMITH
#51 DESERT HELL

ISBN 978-1-61232-654-2

Chapter One

He had ridden Duke out of Yuma, Arizona, long before daybreak to escape the worst of the heat, but at four in the morning the temperature had been approaching one hundred. Now, with dawn streaking across the desert, Clint reined his horse to a standstill and removed his hat. He wiped the sweat from his brow with a sleeve and stared at the wasteland before him, wondering why anyone would live in this desolate country.

But people did—and they were not just some occasional prospectors. The Gunsmith had traveled the length and breadth of Arizona and knew that it was dotted with small mining towns, oases where men, women, and children eked out a living.

Clint preferred the northern part and especially liked Prescott and Flagstaff. Clint replaced his hat, pulling it down low over his eyes to shield them from the rising sun. He looked to the west and saw a line of low, purplish hills shimmering in the distance. How far? Twenty miles? God, he hoped not that far. The temperature was rising fast. It was amazing, he thought, that Hank Tilson had chosen this country to end his illustrious law career.

Clint thought about his friend's crumpled letter, which he had received just a few weeks ago. Hank had always been a quiet, decent fella, maybe too decent. Hank had never taken a bribe or avoided taking the risks that any good lawman faced—and he'd never asked anyone for a favor. But the letter he'd sent had hinted at trouble, perhaps more than Hank figured he could handle by himself. You had to read between the lines and you had to know Hank, but the message for help was there, and it set the Gunsmith into action. He had ridden out of Cedar City, Utah, and wasted damn little time covering the hot country leading down to Yuma.

Clint reached down and unstrapped his canteen. It was running low. He'd used most of it this morning to wet Duke's muzzle and allow the fine black gelding a few precious swallows. The water tasted warm; he took but a swallow, swishing it around his mouth several minutes before swallowing. Damn, but he sure did not like this country!

He strapped the canteen back to his saddle and said, ''Come on, Duke, if we don't reach Desert Springs by noon, we may dry up and blow away.''

The big gelding started forward again, carefully picking its way through the cactus plants. The desert was a hard land and everything in it had to be hard, too, or it would perish. Clint had faced mountain blizzards that would freeze horses in their tracks and he had faced the howling winds that sweep the prairies where the land can be so flat that you had to hug the ground. He had weathered tornados in Oklahoma and killing hail in the Texas Panhandle, but he knew he would rather face any of them than be subjected to the summer heat of the blistering desert. Whatever it was that Hank Tilson needed, Clint figured that he would take care of the matter and get out of this country just as fast as Duke would carry him. The cool Mogollon Plateau awaited just another couple hundred miles to the northeast.

By three o'clock that afternoon, he could not swallow, and just when his spirits were low, he passed over a ridge and saw a miracle—a town with trees. A smile lit his face, and Duke's head lifted and his step quickened.

''Desert Springs,'' the Gunsmith croaked dryly, ''am I ever glad to see you!''

The town was actually pretty. There was a big spring right in the middle of it and a plaza had been set aside where huge cottonwoods shaded benches and hitching posts. Around the plaza were the same kinds of shops and saloons you would find anywhere out west. To the south Clint saw tailings that reminded him of gophers' mounds dotting a lawn. There was a colony of miners living out there in tents and Clint knew that they would have to have their diggings shaded in order to endure this heat. Gold and silver would support this town, and when they were gone, Desert Springs would dry up and blow away.

As he rode in, he saw a stage leaving town and he wished he were on it. He could tie Duke to the back, climb inside, and let it carry him out of his desert hell.

When he entered town, the first thing he did was find a watering trough for Duke to drink from, and then he boarded him at the livery with very specific instructions as to his care and feeding. Duke had the kind of ebony coat that gleamed after it was brushed. Clint enjoyed currying the animal, but not many liverymen felt the same.

"I'll check in on him every day," he said, "and I expect him to be fed well, watered, and brushed."

"Takes time. Time is worth money."

Clint nodded. "You'll be paid for your time."

The liveryman was tall, thin, and in his fifties. He had drooping eyelids and a habit of looking sideways at a man and talking out of the corner of his mouth. Clint did not especially like him, but the other horses boarding here seemed to have received good care. "Promises don't buy hay."

Clint had been about to turn away, but now he reached around and stared the man down. "You'll be well paid," he said. "Now take good care of my horse—or else!"

The man gulped and nodded vigorously. "Yes, sir!" he replied.

Clint relaxed. He was not one to lose his temper, but when it came to the care of Duke, he had a tendency to be a little bit sensitive. "I'm looking for Sheriff Tilson. I rode by his office and saw a closed sign in his window. You know where I might find him?"

The liveryman's eyes dropped to the gun on Clint's hip and

his eyes seemed to read that here was a man who knew how to use a sidearm. "You—" He swallowed nervously. "You one of Red Taggert's men come to empty the sheriff of his belongings?"

"Who is Red Taggert?"

The liveryman relaxed, but there was still a wariness in his droopy eyes. "Hard to believe that you haven't heard of the man," he said.

"Well, I haven't, and if you don't explain to me what the hell the trouble is here and where I can find Hank, I'm going to ruin your day!"

"All right! All right!" he cried out as Clint balled his fists. "I believe you. I just didn't want someone to go over to Hank's place and clean out his belongings yet."

"What do you mean?" Clint demanded. "What's wrong?"

"Hank left yesterday morning early. Word I get is that he got a note from Red Taggert to meet him out in the desert someplace for a showdown—just the two of them."

"I don't believe that," Clint said. "Hank is too smart to fall for something like that."

The liveryman nodded. "Sure, but he didn't have much choice. Four days ago, Red grabbed Mrs. Gottman right off the street and carried her away. She is a respectable woman and her husband has been raising hell ever since and he owns half the businesses here."

"I can understand why he'd be upset. Did Hank get a posse and go after them?"

"Other than Gottman, no one would volunteer."

"What about you?"

The man shook his head. "Got a wife and six kids to feed. Not much sense in riding after Mrs. Gottman and getting killed for another man's wife, is there?"

"So," Clint growled, "Hank and this Gottman fella went out alone."

"That's right. They ain't come back yet, and the betting men in Desert Springs say they won't ever be seen again."

Clint took a deep breath. He stared out at the desert and

saw the heat waves floating over the tortured country. The temperature had shot past one hundred degrees and was still climbing. Even inside the barn it was baking.

"You know which direction they went?"

"Nope, at least not for sure."

"Give me a hint."

"If I was you, which I am glad I am not, I would try to pick up there trail west. They say that's the direction that Red took when he carried Mrs. Gottman away."

"Thanks," Clint said dryly. "Grain and water my horse well between now and sundown."

The man scratched his head and then mopped it with a filthy handkerchief. "How you going to see anything out there at night?"

"Full moon."

"Huh." He looked up at the rafters of the barn as if the moon were to be seen. "Well, I hadn't much noticed."

Clint was walking away, heading for someplace to hole up for the rest of the afternoon and maybe even have a beer and some food, when the liveryman called out to him. "Hey, mister!"

Clint stopped and turned around. "What?"

"Sure wish you'd pay me before you leave Desert Springs tonight. Betting men of this town won't give you much of a chance to come back alive."

"To hell with them," Clint said softly. "I've been whipping long odds all my life."

Chapter Two

It had always amazed the Gunsmith how gossip traveled fast in a small down; Desert Springs was obviously no exception to that rule. Within two hours, men were beginning to close their shops and find an excuse to file into the Double Eagle Saloon and stare at Clint. The second man to come in recognized him as the famous Gunsmith and that started as much of a stampede as was possible in a town the size of Desert Springs.

Clint was in no mood for attention or a bunch of stupid questions. That the very men who had come to gawk at him had been too damned cowardly to join a posse made him even less likely to be sociable. He drank his beer with a scowl on his face. That was evidence enough that he did not wish to be bothered. Once, someone with too much to drink dared to ask him if he would show him his gun, but Clint pinned him with such a hard stare that the fellow withered and staggered away.

Clint remembered the time when Hank Tilson had saved his hide by arriving just before a gunman named Seegar had tried to ambush him. Seegar had faced him in a gunfight two months earlier and been left with a ruined shoulder for his trouble. Even then Clint had thought that he had been too kind in letting the man live, and after the thwarted ambush, he rectified that earlier mistake. But, if it had not been for Hank, he might have been the one left for the wolves to find down in that Colorado gorge instead of

Seegar. It had been fifteen years ago at least and Clint could remember his promise to come running if there was ever a chance to repay the favor.

Well, the chance was now—if it were not already too late. As he sipped beer, he listened to the saloon conversation, and all of it was about Red Taggert and his gang—what they were up to and what the chances were that Gottman would survive to be reunited with his wife. According to popular opinion, there wasn't any chance at all. The sheriff was riding into a trap, and anyone stupid enough to go along with him would also eat a hail of bullets for his dinner.

Apparently, Red Taggert was infamous in the southern part of Arizona. He had a big gang that numbered at least thirty. He robbed the banks of small towns and the stages that carried gold and silver. He was absolutely fearless, and when he had a battle, he usually preferred not to kill his victims unless they were foolish enough to try to retaliate—or they were brave enough to come seeking justice like Sheriff Tilson and Simon Gottman.

Clint was curious about Mrs. Gottman, wondered why she would be specially chosen for abduction. The answer, he was soon to discover, was not quite what Clint had supposed. Jane Gottman was apparently not only the wife of the town's wealthiest merchant and landowner, but also an extremely beautiful woman who was much younger than her husband. There were a few rumors that the woman had married for money, and that now, in the arms of Red, she would at last have a man who could match her physical needs besides inheriting the wealth of her soon-to-be deceased husband. Clint frowned even deeper after hearing this; he was always amazed at not only how fast gossip traveled, but also how tawdry and cheap it became in the process. He doubted that any woman would be stupid or callous enough to allow herself to be abducted into the desert by a band of outlaws in order to lure her husband to his death for an inheritance.

He finished his beer and turned to go. The saloon fell silent when he coldly surveyed everyone and made no attempt to hide his disgust. "I know you have all come to see the Gunsmith, though I can't imagine what the fuss is all about. And I guess you will think it fine to tell anyone who will listen about this affair. But were I any of you, I should keep my silence, for the question men of honor would ask is this: Why didn't you join the Gunsmith if your fellow citizens were in need?"

Clint smiled coldly. "I used to be a lawman and I am sorry to say that I have seen your kind before. That's one of the reasons I quit. Hank Tilson is a hell of a fine man, too fine a man for the likes of Desert Springs."

Clint rode out of Desert Springs an hour before the sun touched the western hills. Despite the long hard trip from Cedar City, he felt rested and determined to find his friend. He galloped down the desert road until he was clear of the town and then he angled off it, searching for the place where Red, followed by Hank and Gottman, had struck out across the land. One thing about this kind of desert; it held the marks of passage a long, long time because there was little rain and the wind did not strip the land wherever there was heavy brush and sage.

Within forty minutes, Clint was on the outlaw's trail and moving west just as the liveryman had supposed. He watched the sun melt against the griddle-hot earth and he prayed for some coolness, but the heat seemed to radiate off the faded land to punish all living things deep into the night.

A full moon guided him in his quest and he did not push Duke any faster than the animal could go. A big owl sailed soundlessly across the full moon and he heard the mournful howling of coyotes resounding from the hillsides. Once, he stampeded something in the brush and his gun was in his hand before he heard the familiar *heehaw* of a burro and then the muted cursing of a prospector interrupted from his night's sleep.

He rode until almost three in the morning. Then he came to a narrow valley and saw the distant glow of a fire several miles away. Clint immediately felt a surge of hope, for he thought that Red Taggert would certainly not be so stupid as to leave a campfire burning as long as there was a possibility of his being pursued. But then he became depressed by the thought that it might also mean that Red had killed Hank and Gottman and believed there was no longer any danger of being followed.

Clint took a deep breath and touched spurs.

He dismounted a mile from the camp, pulled out his Winchester, and checked his gun, even though he knew it was ready. Then, having no idea how many men might be waiting ahead, or even if it was Red or Hank, he started though the brush on foot. The coyotes were still howling louder than ever and Clint took that as an omen that someone was going to die before the night was over.

Chapter Three

Clint stayed low and moved as quickly as he could. When he finally edged in close to the campfire, he saw one sentry. The man was seated at the edge of the small clearing where at least twenty men were rolled up in blankets, and he loosely held a rifle in the crook of his arm; his head kept falling forward onto his chest. He was obviously struggling to stay awake.

Clint studied each of the sleeping figures carefully, trying to figure out if any might be the sheriff, the kidnapped woman, and her husband. His first priority would be Hank because without his help there didn't seem to be much chance of freeing the others. Hell, the Gunsmith thought, even with Hank, the odds would be astronomical. And though it was against his grain, he was seriously thinking the smartest thing to do right now would be to try to free the hostages and just clear out fast. Red Taggert had a small army camped out here.

First things first, Clint thought, now giving up on trying to figure if any of the sleeping figures was his friend. His best chance figured to be in making the sentry tell him what he wanted to know.

Clint removed his Stetson and began to crawl forward, staying low to the ground until he had circled behind the man. That accomplished, he unholstered his gun and moved in

11

slow. The sentry seemed to sense some kind of danger. Clint flattened and the man sat slightly tensed for a moment before he relaxed. Gradually, his eyelids lowered and then his head sank to his chest. He dozed off once again.

There was no sense in hesitating a moment longer; Clint lifted his gun and sprang forward. His gun arced against the firelight and its barrel crashed down on the sentry's skull. The man groaned softly and then slumped forward, but Clint caught him. The man struggled feebly, for Clint had not used enough force to knock him unconscious. He just momentarily stunned him. There was a fine line between really hammering a man and just taking the fight out of him. Clint had been a lawman long enough to have learned just the right pressure and not to use too much and crack his skull as an inexperienced marshal might do; nothing was more pitiful than seeing some poor, rowdy sonofabitch accidentally turned into a vegetable.

Clint clamped one hand over the sentry's mouth and hissed into his ear, "If you want to live, nod your head!"

The man nodded vigorously; he was wide awake now.

"Good. Slow and easy, raise your right hand and if Sheriff Tilson and the Gottmans are here, point them out, the sheriff first. No mistakes, hear?"

The sentry quickly pointed them out, and he was sweating with terror as Clint's gun poked into his ear. "Are you sure?"

Again the head nodded.

"Fine," Clint said, satisfied the man was telling the truth. "You can go back to sleep now."

He raised the gun and brought it back down on the sentry's skull, only a little harder this time. The man grunted and crumpled to the dirt.

In addition to being bound hand and foot, Hank Tilson had been blindfolded, and when Clint knelt over him, even in the semidarkness, it was easy to see that he had been beaten because his face was badly swollen. Clint was just glad to see that the man was alive. He placed his hand over the sheriff's mouth and poked him into wakefulness. The moment Clint tore away the blindfold, Hank recognized him. The sheriff settled right down and his grin was almost as wide as his face when Clint cut his bonds and helped him to his feet.

It was strange standing among twenty or more sleeping outlaws shaking hands with an old and good friend after so many long years and hard trails, but that is what they did. Finally, Clint pulled his hand free and gave Hank the sentry's gun and rifle. He motioned toward the two sleeping figures that the sentry had pointed out and Hank understood immediately that they were the Gottmans.

Overhead, the moon passed behind a cloud and it suddenly became very dark. Clint edged forward and knelt beside the sleeping figure of Simon Gottman. Clint's fingers groped for his face. He wanted to clamp a hand over Gottman's mouth to prevent a startled outcry before he started to untie his hands and feet.

Clint's palm brushed the man's chin, then he covered the mouth, and that was when all hell broke loose. Gottman wasn't tied at all! In fact, as the man came awake fighting like a wildcat, Clint had the sick feeling he wasn't waking Gottman at all!

"Sonofabitch!" the man coughed out as he drove a fist into Clint's belly and almost bit his hand off. "Sonofabitch!"

Clint pulled his injured hand free and swore. He could hear shouts and then the camp was in mass confusion. The man he was grappling with was trying to reach his throat and Clint could tell by the thick calluses on his powerful hands that this was no city merchant. The sentry had deliberately lied!

Some fool opened fire in the night and Clint hit the ground as bullets screamed across the sage. He heard a woman cry out very close by and he lunged to his feet and threw himself at her. When their bodies collided, he figured he had Mrs. Gottman in his arms because she was soft and probably the only woman in the camp. When she tried to beat at him, there was not a man's strength in her blows.

"Clint!"

It was Sheriff Tilson and now the man was firing as, overhead, the moon was breaking through the clouds again. Clint didn't have time to calm the woman. There was no time to explain that he was not trying to hurt, but rather help her. With regret Clint gave her a hard belt alongside the jaw that dropped her. He picked her up and sprinted for cover with bullets flying in every direction.

They slammed into the brush and Clint was surprised to see that his old friend was right behind him covering his back.

"Where are the horses?" Tilson shouted. "We better get out of here!"

"Horses." Clint took a deep breath. What he had to say next was not going to impress his old lawman friend one damn bit. "I'm afraid all we got is Duke."

The sheriff nailed one of Red Taggert's gang who thought it might be a good idea to play hero. Then the sheriff yelled, "Where is this Duke? He bringing the horses?"

The Gunsmith drilled another man, who went down and did not move. "Nope. Duke is my horse. There isn't any other."

Sheriff Hank Tilson ducked his head behind a rock and stared at Clint with disbelief. "You must be kidding, Clint! You come out here to rescue us or get us riddled?"

Clint shrugged. This was one time when he just did not have a good answer. He saw another outlaw charge forward and he shot him cleanly.

Tilson rolled back to face the gang. "Well," he said philosophically, "at least now I got a chance to take a few of them with me."

Clint smiled. "That's the Hank Tilson I admire."

"Go to hell," Hank drawled with a grin.

"Can't. We're already there."

Clint looked up at the stars. He guessed it was about five in the morning. Another hour or so and it would be daylight.

They had better be gone from this place or things would go from bad to worse.

And things were, he had a hunch, going to get a whole lot worse before they got any better.

Chapter Four

"Where is your husband!" Clint shouted at the woman.

Looking dazed, Jane Gottman shook her head and Clint figured she had every right to be. The way things had turned out, it was a miracle that the three of them were still alive.

"He must still be tied up and in there among them," Hank said. "Knowing Red, I'd say the chances are damned slim her husband is still alive."

"No," she whispered. "Red may be bad, but he would not execute anyone. He is not a cold-blooded killer."

Both Clint and the sheriff glanced at her quizzically and then returned gunfire in the direction of the outlaw camp. The Gunsmith had no time to consider her words, but it did seem mighty strange that under these circumstances, Mrs. Gottman would stick up for the leader of the outlaw band.

The sheriff looked around. "We have to get horses. If we try to run, they'll come and hunt us down at daybreak. I don't mind dying so much, but not on the run."

"I'll try for some horses," the Gunsmith said.

"Nope, it's my job. I'm the one who is paid to risk his hide. Red Taggert is my problem, not yours."

"Fine," Clint said, "but I had a notion that he was the reason you might have sent for me."

"Forget that for now," Hank said. "I think I've got a decent plan to get us out of here."

Just then a bullet whistled by Clint's face, and he flattened and rolled sideways before he came up and fired a couple of

17

rounds. Then he ducked again and reloaded.

"You and the girl find that horse of yours," Hank said, "while I cover you. Then sneak in among them and steal a couple of their horses."

Clint snorted. "Just as easy as that, huh?"

"Yep."

"No dice," Clint said.

"I've lived fifteen years longer than you. That means I have less time on this earth to lose if my plan doesn't work."

"Oh, damn it!" Jane shouted at them. "Are you both going to sit here and argue while my husband is out there somewhere among them?"

Clint finished loading his gun and scowled. He had no intention of letting Hank Tilson cover his back and remain to face however many of Red Taggert's gang were still in fighting shape. "I'm staying," he said stubbornly. "What you do is your own business."

"Damn it anyway!" Tilson said, emptying his gun.

"You both had better stay and let me ride for help," the woman said impatiently. "I can tell both of you mules aren't about to budge an inch."

Clint nodded. "That seems like a reasonable enough solution. But I'll have to take you and put you in the saddle 'cause without me Duke wouldn't let you near him."

"Then quit palaverin' and do it!" Hank said. "In the meantime, I'll circle and try to slip in among them and grab two horses."

"How the hell will I be able to pick you out from all of them?"

Hank Tilson scratched his head and then fingered his swollen face. "I'll be the ugliest," he said. And before Clint could protest that there was not time to study a man's face before deciding whether to shoot him, Hank Tilson was moving away.

"Come on," Clint hissed. "Let's get you out of here."

The young woman did not protest, but neither did she seem to be in a particular hurry either. She seemed, well, almost reluctant to go, yet Clint did not think that it was because of concern for her husband.

"I can shoot a gun or a rifle," she told him as he hurried her along. "I'm not afraid to fight for my life."

He glanced sideways at her in the moonlight. She was under thirty; tall, with high cheekbones and honey-blond hair. The woman was still pretty despite what she must have been through these past few days with Red Taggert. She was dressed in a man's shirt and pants; both were ridiculously baggy every place on her except in the chest, for Jane was a very well-endowed woman.

"Did you hear me? I said I was not afraid to fight beside you."

"I heard," he said, pulling her along at a trot and seeing Duke just up ahead. "But we need more help than you could give."

She snorted with derision and her face went hard. "Help from who? The townspeople? They're all a bunch of cowards. Red and his gang own this part of the country. No one has the guts to stand up to them."

"You're wrong. There are three of us."

"Who is the third?"

"Your husband."

Jane grabbed the saddle and Clint watched her mount Duke. For a moment when she had been swinging her leg over, he had caught the outline of a very shapely pair of hips. Very shapely.

She looked down at him. "You must think I am a real bitch, but I am going to tell you this anyway. Sheriff Tilson might just have been able to sneak into camp and get me free except for my husband. Simon froze, and then when a sentry called out, he started running like a damned rabbit. The sentry opened fire and would have killed him if Tilson hadn't stopped him. But by then, it was all over and Red had both of them caught."

Clint looked up at her. She was really beautiful, but right now her face was like granite, no softness to it at all. "Hank

Tilson and I are fighting men; your husband is not. You shouldn't be too hard on him, Mrs. Gottman. After all, he came.''

"He had a lot to lose. What's your excuse?"

"I don't need one," Clint replied.

"I know. And *that* is the difference." She lifted the reins. "I won't even get back to town until noon. There is no telling if I can shame anyone into coming to help."

"Try," Clint said.

She reached down and touched his face. "Why is it that the brave, handsome ones like you always die young?"

"Get the hell out of here," Clint said roughly. "As long as Hank and I have bullets, the dying is going to be pretty one-sided, and it won't be us."

She smiled. "I won't forget you. And here's some advice: If it comes down to your life or Simon's, for my money, you are worth a whole lot more."

Jane wheeled the big gelding and galloped away then. The Gunsmith spun around and headed back toward the battle. He would have liked to have had a chance to know why that woman felt nothing but contempt for her husband and had defended the character of a notorious outlaw. None of it made sense. But then, sense counted for nothing when it came to doing or dying.

Chapter Five

Clint circled the camp. It was his intention to try to get in
among the outlaw band while it was still dark. He glanced up
at the moon hoping for more clouds. There were some, but it
would take a little luck and a little time before he might be
able to expect any help, and by then dawn would be breaking
over the eastern horizon.

No matter what happened, he and Hank needed to be on
horseback and riding like hell back to Desert Springs come
daylight. If Jane Gottman were successful, they'd meet help,
and if she were not successful, well, they'd bring that outlaw
band right into town and make the people fight to defend their
homes and businesses. It was amazing how, when a man had
something of his own at stake, he often discovered he did
have a backbone.

Clint heard the crack of a bullet and he dived for cover and
then crawled until he came to the body of an outlaw. The man
had a black vest and a hat and Clint put them both on. Then he
moved quickly into the clearing just as boldly as if he be-
longed there. He joined the others firing into the brush, and
even though he expected to get a bullet in the back every
single moment, he did not.

It seemed obvious that Hank was doing a hell of a fine job
raising confusion. He was moving to the left—firing, rolling,
and then coming up to do it all over again. Several more of
Red's gang were down. Most were winged, but a couple
looked dead. Clint saw the horses and his first thought was to
get to them, but then he realized he would stand no chance at

all of reaching Hank alive. As soon as the horses stampeded, the gang would realize the plan and attack his friend.

I'll have to get Red Taggert, he thought, moving toward the center of the outlaw resistance and trying to keep his hat low over his eyes and at the same time not make himself a target for one of the sheriff's bullets.

Red Taggert was easy to spot. The man was well over six feet tall and shouting orders at his men, telling them to stay low and pick their shots. Clint moved in right behind him and then, because he could think of no better way to do it, he just jammed his gun into Red's side and whispered, "We're backing out of this fight a step at a time. Then you are calling off your dogs."

The outlaw leader stiffened and dared not look around. "That you, Simon, you bastard?"

"Nope," Clint said. "And you have two seconds to do what I say or you're going to meet your maker."

"I don't believe you," he choked out with hatred. "Whoever you are, I'm your only ticket out of this alive. Shoot me and you'll follow me to hell."

Clint had to give the outlaw credit for brains because what he said was, unfortunately, closer to the truth than he cared to admit. Still, Clint knew that he had to be strong and, that if Red sensed any hesitation, he was finished anyway. He cocked his gun right next to Red's right ear. "I'll count to two out loud and then you are meat. One . . ."

"Wait! Don't shoot, you crazy bastard!"

"Then back up!"

This time, Red Taggert cooperated, and when they were behind the line of rocks that his men were using as cover, Clint yanked him to his feet and shoved his gun into his spine. "Now, tell them to drop their guns."

"They won't do it."

"Beg them!"

"Hold your fire!" Red shouted over the din. "Hold your fire!"

The outlaw guns fell silent and they all turned their

weapons on Clint. Out in the brush and cactus, the sheriff's voice boomed, "You did it, Gunsmith!"

"If if were you, Hank, I would not start the celebration yet."

Hank Tilson had never listened to anyone's advice in his entire life and he wasn't going to start doing so now. With a grin on his face, he came marching into view.

"Look out, sheriff!"

Clint saw a man in a soiled suit jump toward Hank and then his gun swiveled toward one of the outlaws who was making his play, but was already too late. The outlaw's first bullet twisted Hank around and his second slammed Simon Gottman over backward. Clint triggered a slug into the outlaw's chest, killing him instantly.

Clint placed his gun against Red's temple and growled, "Next man who does something stupid like that dies. Then I shoot Red." When he was certain no more fools were ready to die, Clint reached to feel Simon Gottman's pulse. There just wasn't any.

"That poor, stupid bastard," Red growled. "I never would have guessed he had guts enough to do something like that to save someone else's life."

"Neither would his wife," Clint said.

"Tell your men to throw down their guns."

"Uh-uh," Red grunted as Clint jammed his own gun painfully into the outlaw's spine. "You can kill me right now. I won't tell them to do it. They'd hang and they know it if they went to trial. They are all wanted men, most for murder."

"It would seem we have a little problem then," Clint said. "One without an easy solution."

"There is a solution. Turn us all loose and we will let you go."

"I wasn't born yesterday and you aren't a man of the cross," Clint said.

"Then let me go and I will promise you no trouble on the way back to Desert Springs. There's wounded men here, one of the worst being your friend.''

Clint stared at Hank and realized that the man was now on his feet with a bullet in the shoulder. ''How bad is it, Hank?''

''It'll hold until I get to a doctor.''

''The hell it will,'' Red spat. ''The man is bleeding to death. Make up your mind, Gunsmith.''

Clint was not one to make deals with outlaws and murderers, but this time would be the exception. ''All right. Tell them to gather their own wounded and to clear out of here fast, before I change my mind.''

Red laughed harshly. ''Hell, you mean before *I* change my mind. Boys, you can get on your horses and ride free. Take all the wounded who can make it. Leave the rest for the town doctor to fix up for hanging.''

''We'll leave nobody still breathing,'' came a snarl.

Red nodded. He looked at his men. ''Jeb was a fool to open fire a minute ago and he almost got me killed along with himself. I want all of you to ride on out and don't try to stop them from taking me to jail. But if there is to be a hanging, you all come and burn Desert Springs to the damn ground. You kill the jury and you rape their wives. Hear me!''

''We hear you!'' they shouted.

''Good.'' Red turned back to face Clint and the sheriff. ''I hope you also heard.''

Clint nodded. He did not quite know what to say. By the looks of this crowd, they could destroy the town. When he glanced at the sheriff, he knew that Hank was in no shape to stop them. So what was to happen to Red Taggert? Was he to be tried and sentenced to hang?

''One way or another,'' Clint said softly, ''you are going to get what you have coming.''

Taggert chuckled almost good-naturedly. ''In case you haven't heard, Desert Springs is a betting town. Don't be too surprised when you discover that the odds against me going to the gallows are longer than they are that you have stepped into a whole lot more than you bargained for, Gunsmith.''

Clint was about to tell him the same as he had the

liveryman—that he had always fought and won against long odds. But just then Hank Tilson collapsed. Suddenly, the odds seemed insurmountable.

Chapter Six

"Freeze!" Clint shouted just after Hank Tilson hit the earth. "If anyone moves, I'll drill him first and Red second!" Clint knew that he wasn't bluffing, and perhaps because the outlaw band knew that he was the Gunsmith, they figured that he was serious, and they did not want to risk Red's life.

He had a forearm locked around Red's neck and the man choked out, "Do as he says!"

The wildness bled out of them and Clint knew that he had won a momentary victory. He ordered the outlaws to bring four horses; one for Mr. Gottman whose body would be lashed across the saddle, one for Hank after his wound had been covered by a bandage, and the final two for Red and himself. After he had the horses and they were set to leave, he stampeded their horses and figured they had best get the hell out of there. If it were for Hank, he might have tried to bring in the lot of them, but that would have likely led to a bloodbath. He decided to wait for another time and place.

It wasn't until they were miles away and behind a bench of hills that Clint finally allowed himself to breathe normally again.

"You may think you beat us," Red drawled, "but the battle is just beginning. I will never even go to trial in Desert Springs."

"I wouldn't be too sure of that."

Red shrugged. "Even if I did go to trial, I'd be set free."

Clint looked at him sharply. "How do you figure that?"

"I got connections," Red said with a confident grin. "The

27

judge and any jury would realize that to sentence me to the gallows would be like signing their own death sentences. You've been a lawman for many years, one of the best. Don't tell me you haven't seen your share of rigged juries and spineless judges.''

Clint untied a rope from one of the saddles. He fashioned a noose and reached out and tore Red's hat off. Then he slipped the noose over the man's shock of red hair and roughly tightened it around his neck.

''What the hell you doing!''

Clint said, ''I've taken many a killer and outlaw back to town to face a judge and a jury. When we ride into Desert Springs, I want those people to know without question that you are going to hang for your crimes.''

The man sneered. ''Before this is all over, Gunsmith, I'll nail your hide to the barn door and then I'll . . . ahhh!''

Clint had yanked the rope hard and it gave him a lot of satisfaction seeing Red's face turn purple.

He eased the tension, and when the man opened his mouth to curse, Clint yanked the rope again. After that, Red Taggert kept his mouth shut and his thoughts to himself, for he knew that Clint would break him just as he would a horse of its bad habits.

Five miles out, Hank Tilson stirred and Clint dismounted. He checked the shoulder bandage, and it seemed to have worked well enough to stop the bleeding. Clint helped his friend sit up in the saddle.

''What happened?'' Tilson grunted. He was sweating profusely and was as white as a cloud.

Clint told him in swift, clipped sentences and ended by repeating Red's smug prediction that he would not go to trial and that even if he did he would be set free by a cowardly jury and judge.

''The bastard is probably right,'' Tilson said through clenched teeth. ''There is nobody in that town with any backbone.''

"Simon Gottman and his wife must have been the exceptions."

Tilson nodded. "Simon was a lot braver than any of us thought. I always knew that Jane had a lot of grit. She's a fighter."

Red laughed crudely. "She's not bad naked on a blanket either!"

Clint yanked the rope so hard that Red was almost toppled from his saddle. He nearly chocked to death before Clint gave him some slack and warned, "Next time you say something about a lady and the widow of the man whose death you are responsible for, I will hang you myself!"

"Easy, Clint!"

"Easy, hell," the Gunsmith responded. "I'm forming a deep and abiding dislike for this man. watching him swing from a rope is going to be worth riding down here into this hell."

The sheriff looked away. His eyes were etched with pain and worry. He looked older than his some fifty years this morning. "Hank?"

"Yeah?"

"When this is over, why don't you pack up and leave this desert? From what I have seen of the desert and the town, those folks don't deserve a man as good as you and the desert hates everyone."

He shrugged. "There are some good folks here. And I can't do much about the desert."

"I didn't meet any good ones in the saloon when I asked for a posse to help. I guess you didn't either or you'd have brought more than Gottman to try to rescue the woman."

"Those people can be strong when they have to, Clint."

"We'll see," he answered, not believing it for a minute. "All we need for a jury is honest men who aren't afraid of reaching a just verdict. And if they won't do their job, then I aim to take things into my own hands."

Both Hank and Red Taggert were shocked. The sheriff

said, "I don't like the sound of that, Clint. What are you trying to say?"

"Just this. I intend to see this sonofabitch either sentenced to a long term in prison or, better yet, hung outright. If a Desert Springs judge and jury can't see to that, then I will escort this prisoner out of the town and find a federal judge and a marshal and he'll be tried in Phoenix or Tucson or wherever in order to get the job done."

"Are you going over my head?" Tilson looked wounded.

"If I have to," Clint said stubbornly. "Besides a murder charge, there is kidnapping and rape. Seems to me, Hank, there isn't much question about a verdict. Why are you hedging?"

The sheriff shrugged, took a deep breath, and let it out slowly. "Is that what I am doing? Maybe I'm just getting old and scared. Maybe that's what happens to a lawman who has been on the job too damn long."

"Uh-uh," the Gunsmith grunted. "Scared men don't head out, two against twenty, to save a woman."

"Twenty years ago, I'd have pulled it off," Hank said quietly.

"Maybe. The fact of the matter is, I didn't do such a great job myself. But that doesn't change the fact that this man needs his neck stretched."

"Hell, I didn't kill Gottman! You both saw that," Red spat out. "So what is this talk about hanging?"

"Kidnapping and rape are hanging offenses."

Red smiled. "You ever think that the Gottman woman might have wanted me to take her away and use her?"

Clint started to yank the noose, but Red squealed, "Wait! I'm telling the truth! You—you think I just happened to come upon her in the street that afternoon? Hell, no, she was waiting to meet me!"

"You are lying!" Hank Tilson snarled.

Tilson shook his head. "She wanted a young, hard man for a change, and I was the one she chose.

"Oh, she'll deny it now, but it's true and before any jury

convicts me, you'll have to prove I ain't lying. She'll have to get up on the witness stand to tell the jury all about what happened and she won't do that!''

The Gunsmith's lips curled with contempt. ''The next thing you'll be telling us is that she wanted her husband to be killed so that she could have all his money and property.''

''That's right!'' Red cried. ''That's exactly what she did want to happen.''

Hank Tilson managed to find the strength to grab the rope out of Clint's hand. He wrapped it around the pommel and spurred his horse into a run. Red Taggert shrieked in fear and spurred his own horse, knowing that if he did not his neck would be popped and broken.

Clint hesitated for only one moment. He remembered how Jane Gottman had, for some reason, momentarily defended Red's character. Was the man actually telling the truth? If there were any doubt . . . ''Damn it!'' Clint cussed, ''I guess I better keep the man alive just long enough to find out!''

As he spurred after the wounded old lawman, who was trying to kill his prisoner, Clint made one promise to himself and that was that he was going to pay a little visit to the Gottman widow. When he did, he was going to have some hard questions to ask. There was just the slimmest possibility that Red Taggert was telling the truth and then there might be two people standing trial instead of one.

Chapter Seven

In Desert Springs the first place they went to was the doctor's. He confirmed what Clint already knew; the bullet had passed cleanly through Hank's right shoulder and the wound would heal, but that would take time and Hank might always experience pain. Even more important, his days of the fast draw were over. He could still use a gun better than most, but he'd be considerably slower at it, and that was an invitation to death in his profession. Like it or not, Hank's days of being a lawman were finished.

Clint locked Red Taggert in jail and told a dozen onlookers to stand guard. He then headed for the undertaker's parlor to make sure that Simon Gottman was being properly taken care of and that the funeral arrangements were being handled by someone. Gottman had shouted a warning that might have saved the Gunsmith's life and Clint felt a sense of obligation. Gottman had lost his courage earlier and gotten the sheriff in a jam. He apparently tried to atone for that.

When Clint reached the undertaker's office, he stopped at the entrance. He saw Mrs. Gottman dressed in a black dress and appearing a whole lot handsomer than a newly widowed woman had a right to appear.

"One hundred dollars is ridiculous!" she cried, unaware of Clint's presence. "Just because my husband owned a great deal of property here doesn't mean that I am going to let you and every other opportunist in Desert Springs fleece me!"

"Mrs. Gottman," the thin, ascerbic-looking undertaker

33

wheezed, "believe me, I share your sense of sorrow and deep loss, and I am only trying to make this tragic occasion as easy and painless for you as is humanly possible."

Jane Gottman did not believe a word of it. "Then I want you to have a simple funeral ceremony. My husband was not a loved man in this community. Am I not correct to say that to you, Mr. Wadle? And didn't he have a most terrible argument only last week because of your continual tardiness in paying your rent?"

"My dear Mrs. Gottman! Please!" he begged, touching the back of his thin hand to his pale forehead in a gesture that was almost theatrical. "This is certainly not the time or the place to discuss crass details such as money."

"Then when is the time or place?" she stormed. "No, Mr. Wadle, we will settle this matter right now. Instead of that fancy coffin with the solid silver handles, I think my deceased husband would be every bit as comfortable in a simple pine box."

The undertaker paled. His hand fluttered to his goatee, and he stammered, "Surely you don't mean one of those!" He pointed to a stack of what looked to Clint like rifle packing cases.

"That's exactly what I mean. How much are they?"

"I charge the county five dollars to buy criminals and paupers without relatives who . . ."

"Five dollars it is then," she said, taking it out of her purse and shoving it into the undertaker's hands. "And I expect a few good words over him tomorrow."

"But—but this is scandalous!" The man erupted in an unexpected show of anger. "Absolutely outrageous! Your husband was the wealthiest man in this town and you are having him buried as though he were a—a penniless beggar!"

"God will judge—not you, me, or a bunch of hypocrites who hadn't the guts to accompany him and Sheriff Tilson when they tried to rescue me and bring Red Taggert to justice."

She swung around and collided with Clint who had been standing in the doorway listening with interest.

"Excuse me!" she said, sweeping past him.

Clint took off after her as she threaded her way through the pedestrians. Everyone they passed stopped and turned and then began to gossip. Back at the undertaker's parlor, Mr. Wadle was shouting that she would be sorry, that she was forever disgracing her name and her reputation.

It was obvious that the widow did not care. She stomped on with her back stiff and her eyes straight ahead until she came to a lovely home with a white picket fence covered with roses.

"Mrs. Gottman, I need to speak with you!" he called.

At the door she turned and now Clint saw that she was crying; tears were streaming down her pretty face. She looked at him as if seeing him for the first time, and then she nodded once very formally. Clint wiped his boot on the doormat and followed her inside.

The room was anything but what he what he might have expected to find in the home of a wealthy man. The place was threadbare. The rugs in the hallway were worn through, the paint was yellowed with age, the furniture was dull and worn, and some of the tables had been put together with great crudeness.

Jane Gottman marched to a bureau and pulled out a cheap decanter of brandy. She rummaged in a drawer and found a couple of glasses. Then wordlessly she led him to a closed door and pushed it open so they could enter a library.

It was semidark, for the curtains were drawn, but once Clint's eyes grew accustomed to the faint light, he whistled with appreciation because the library was huge and impressive. In it reposed elegant furniture, statues of jade and hand-painted china, Persian rugs, and collections of Shakespeare and the finest writers and philosophers. To Clint, it was like stepping out of a poor country hovel into a realm of class and nobility. "Your husband, he seemed to care very little about the appearance of your house, for the outward show or appearance of it. He must have loved this room, though.''

Her eyes flashed. ''No,'' she whispered, pouring two glasses full and handing him one. ''This room is mine! It is my world, the only beauty in this entire hellish desert and the bedrock of my sanity. What you see here is me!''

He studied her. ''You've read all these books?''

Now, finally, she smiled. ''I confess to having read only a dozen of them, but those I have practically learned by heart. Shakespeare, Longfellow, Kipling, their words I cherish. But even had I not read a single tome, I would still treasure them all, for I think them very beautiful. Besides, must a person constantly study a painting to know its true value?''

''No.'' Clint took a drink of the brandy. He motioned out toward the shabby parlor through which they had just passed. ''I don't understand any of this. Out there, his world; in here, your own.''

''Then let me tell you,'' she said, tossing her drink down and pouring another. ''I married my husband for money. Does that shock you—''

''Adams. Clint Adams. And no, there is very little that shocks me in this world. I have seen and heard almost everything in my years as a lawman. Money is a good reason to marry, probably a lot better reason than most. I am just surprised that you are honest enough to admit your true motive.''

''Why not be honest? I have nothing to hide. You cannot hide anything in a small, miserable town like Desert Springs. Everyone knows everything about everyone. There is no privacy, not even in your own bedroom. Only . . .''—and she emphasized the word with exaggerated slowness—''only in this room could I lock out the real world and no one could penetrate inside. Not even poor, stingy, money-grubbing Simon who loved to accumulate wealth and to manipulate the lives of small people.''

''Why did you allow me in here?'' he asked bluntly.

"Why not keep me in the parlor? Or, for that matter, why invite me into your home at all?"

She studied him, her glass touching her full lips. Jane Gottman seemed to make a decision. "All right," she said a little loudly. "Since this is my day of truth, I shall tell you. I allowed you in here because you came to help rescue me from Red Taggert and you had absolutely nothing to gain by doing it. I found that absolutely fascinating."

He frowned. "The sheriff came to rescue you."

"It was his job. If he had not done so, my husband would have financed his ouster from office. He could easily have gotten the man fired."

She smiled. Poured them both another glass of brandy. "Why did you do it?"

"Hank once saved my life. I owe him."

If she were disappointed, it did not show. "And what about me? Would you have ridden out just for me?"

He thought about that one for a moment. "Yes," he said. "If no one else would have gone, then I would have come alone."

"Rather foolish, wouldn't you say, one against twenty? As you must have guessed, when I returned on your wonderful horse, I was unable to enlist the help of anyone to return to your aid. They are cowards and weak gossipy men who look at me with the eyes of lions and the hearts of kittens."

Clint could not hide a smile and wondered if that was some line she had gotten out of a book of poetry or if she had created it on her own.

She moved closer to him and set her brandy down on the table. "When a man risks his life for me without thought of reward, I . . . I find that very, very gallant. I feel . . ."— she reached up and her long, supple fingers played with the hair at the nape of his neck as she whispered into his ear— "very, very grateful."

Clint did not know quite what to say.

"And I want to repay you every way that I can."

"It's not . . ." He was going to tell her that he had not expected reward of any kind, but her lips covered his own and then her other hand was unbuttoning his fly and slipping into his pants.

"It's not what?" she murmured as she found his manhood and began to run her fingers up and down it, making it grow hard and long.

"I forgot," he said, placing his own drink on the marble-top table, spilling it, but not caring. He could not believe that he was in a room like this in the middle of a damned desert and that the woman who was stroking his cock was a widow dressed in black. Lovely and voluptuous, she was a widow whose husband was yet lying on the mortician's table and that gave Clint pause.

A flash of guilt overcame him and he pushed away from her for a moment. "Listen," he said in a voice hoarse with his own passion, "I know you are very upset by what happened to you out there with those outlaws, and then your husband getting himself killed and everything, and I wonder if maybe you ought to think a minute before you go any further. You might not be thinking very clearly and I don't want you to be filled with remorse an hour from now."

She stepped back and began to unbutton her bodice; the black satin dress opened to reveal creamy white skin. Her bra of black satin was straining, and when she unclasped it and her firm, bulging breasts pushed free, the nipples were dark and hard.

Jane watched his face, saw the hunger, and smiled. "My husband was a miser and he saved all of his money, except what I made him spend on this library for me. He saved everything, even me. Do you understand what I am saying, Mr. Adams?"

He nodded, not trusting his voice because his blood was pounding and his mouth was dry. She had the most beautiful breasts he had seen in a long, long while, and as he watched, she began to slip the mourning dress off to reveal a most mouth-watering sight.

He understood perfectly. No further explanations were necessary or even welcome. Clint reached down and unstrapped his gun. He closed and latched the library door behind him. A man could learn a lot from all these great books; a man could also learn something between those long, silky legs of the widow Gottman.

Chapter Eight

Jane licked her lips as she finished removing her clothing. "I felt like a hypocrite," she whispered, coming to him. "I never wanted my husband, not the way I want you right now."

He shucked his boots and pants and then his underwear. She watched him with an animal hunger. When he reached out and caught her nipples between his thumbs and forefingers and rolled them gently, she gasped with pleasure, and her head lolled back toward her milky white shoulders. Jane tossed her golden hair and reached for his erection. Finding it, she smiled and then pulled him to her.

Her mouth opened and he captured it with his as she bent slightly and began to rub his swollen cock up and down against her. He could feel that she was wet and hot, and it was all Clint could do to keep from jamming himself into her and exploding.

"Feels good," she whispered, breathing hard. "Oh, does it ever feel good!"

He laughed softly. "It's about to feel even better, Mrs. Gottman."

"Jane," she moaned, "I have always been just Jane to my friends and you are definitely my friend."

He reached down and cupped her buttocks. He lifted her to her toes and drove his swollen cock deep into her. She moaned and shuddered. She began to hunch and grind and he kissed her hard, his own tongue urgent and insistent. Their bodies were grinding against one another, round and round, then in and out, and he could hear the soft, slick, slurping sound of their union. "The desk," she whispered, "take me on the desk!"

He tore his lip away and glanced over at the big mahogany writing desk. It was obviously strong enough to support their weight, but it was covered with papers and writing materials. "But Jane . . ." he began.

She pulled away and then began kissing his chest. Her lips traced down to his wet cock, and she took it into her mouth and began to suck it with immense pleasure. Clint placed his hands alongside her face and let her take all the time that she wanted. Finally, when he could stand it no longer and a fire was building deep in his loins, he pulled her to her feet and then led her to the desk. With one sweep of his arm, he cleared the top and laid her down on it. Then he climbed up and mounted her with fierce urgency.

"Yes!" she cried, reaching around and digging her nails into his buttocks, pulling him roughly back into her. Her eyes rolled and perspiration beaded on her forehead and then across her huge breasts as he pumped her harder and harder. "Oh, oh, now!" she screamed as her body began to jerk and her gasps became hoarse, unintelligible cries.

Clint's powerful body began to spasm and his cock pistoned in and out with incredible force and speed. He gritted his teeth and then pinned her to the desk as his body stiffened and he was filling her with his seed. She was crying, begging him for more, for all of it, as she lost complete control of her own lovely body and her heels drummed wildly on the desk. She screamed out in ecstasy.

He lifted her off the desk and carried her to a small settee because she was too weak to stand. He poured drinks, and when he caught his breath, he said, "For a woman who says she was never used, you sure have a lot of talent."

That pleased her. He knew it would. "Thanks, Clint. You are pretty special yourself. I can tell you have had a lot of women." Her cheeks colored, and she studied her glass, avoiding his eyes. "How . . . how do I compare?"

The question was asked so shyly that Clint knew it had been extremely difficult, and it was easy to tell her the truth. "You are one of the very best," he said. "You stand behind no woman I have ever had and that is the pure and honest truth of the matter. Any man would crawl over hot coals to climb between your legs, Jane."

Her chest swelled with pride. "Thank you," she said, looking into his eyes. "Thank you very much. You see, with Simon it was so infrequent, and when he did do it to me, he was so . . ." She shook her head, searching for the right word to convey her meaning. "He was so economical. He just seemed to be saving himself all the time. After a while, I began to wonder if it was me or what, and if it was ever going to be any good."

Clint nodded. He had heard versions of this same story a hundred times—tales of women who had been practically ruined by selfish men who cared nothing but for their own carnal pleasure and did not even realize that a woman could feel the same ecstasy as a man if she were handled right.

But there was something else that was on Clint's mind, something that he had to get out into the open. "Jane, I have to ask you a question and I want a straight answer."

She lifted her head, stung by the implication that she might be inclined to lie to him.

"What I want to know," he said, doggedly determined to finish, "is if you wanted to be kidnapped by Red Taggert? Did you and he plan it?"

Jane's eyes flashed. She downed her brandy in a single gulp and snapped, "Whatever gave you that kind of stupid idea?"

"Red. He was bragging that you wanted him to take you away. He pointed out that, if your husband came after you, he would be easy to kill and that would make you a very wealthy widow. And that is exactly how it turned out."

She refilled both of their glasses, and he noticed that when she poured, the bottle rattled on the glass rims. "Clint," she said finally, "I think we have the beginning of a wonderful time together. I am wealthy now, and I am not stingy like my late husband. As I said earlier, I appreciate your courage and I will reward it. What just happened a few minutes ago is a small sample of the rewards I have in mind.''

He smiled. ''I'll take you anytime, but never would I live off a woman.''

''Good! A man of pride. I like that!''

''You never answered my question,'' he said. ''What about you and Red?''

''He kidnapped me and raped me repeatedly and savagely. He is a man like you—only he is a pig, one who thinks only of his pleasure. He is rough and I fought him.''

''You may have to testify to that fact.''

She took a deep breath and let it out slowly. ''Then I will be equal to the task,'' she said in a trembling voice. ''That man is an animal and, because of him, my husband is dead. Never mind that I did not love Simon. That is not an issue in the sentencing, is it?''

''No.''

''Red Taggert is a murderer, a kidnapper, and a rapist. What he did to me in front of his men was unspeakable and disgusting. I do not want it to happen to some other poor woman. I will do everything in my power to see that he is sentenced to hang.''

Clint nodded. That was all he needed to know. Without this woman's testimony, Taggert might go free, or at the worst receive a slap on the wrist, serve a short jail sentence, and then be turned loose.

Jane stood up and went to stand before him. ''Do you think I am desirable?'' she asked quietly.

''Your husband never told you?''

''No,'' she whispered, ''he would not.''

Clint reached out and pulled her to him. Jane Gottman was a strange and complicated young woman, also one who was beautiful and passionate. She bore scars, deep ones, and he decided he might be able to help remove some of them. It would be fun trying, he thought, as he ran his hands down her sleek flanks. He heard her sharp intake of breath as his fingers probed her hidden places.

"You are very desirable," he told her as his lips traced the contours of one bare shoulder. "And I am going to make you believe that if it takes the rest of this day and the night."

"It might take even longer," she breathed, reaching for him, her hands beginning to massage his cock into fresh, throbbing excitement.

Clint picked her up and headed for the door. Somewhere in this house there had to be a real bed, and if he were correct about what lay in store during the hours to come, they definitely needed a real bed.

Chapter Nine

It took seven days to pick a jury, and even then no one wanted to serve on it. Only when Clint had paid each prospective juror a visit to ask for their help was it possible to go to trial. Clint had absolutely no confidence in the jurors. They had demonstrated that they neither wanted to serve nor believed that sticking their necks out for the sake of justice would have any other result than getting their heads chopped off.

The judge was no more encouraging. He was a chubby man with protruding ears, glasses that kept slipping down a red nose, and eyes that were rheumy and bloodshot. He seemed a despot, a man who dispensed the law for the sole reason of fattening his own wallet. He looked as if he could be bought for the price of a bottle of gin.

Hank Tilson was the first to take the witness stand. He told the packed courtroom about the lawlessness of Red Taggert, how his gang and been running roughshod across southern and central Arizona for a number of years, and how, even though he and his men always wore some type of mask it was obvious they were guilty as sin. He pointed out that Red could not keep a large gang of free-spending outlaws in grub, women, and whiskey by raising corn and potatoes.

Hank's dry humor caused an outburst of laughter, but it quickly evaporated when Red's lawyer pointed out that the issue was not the source of Red's income, but rather his guilt or innocence of murder as charged. Even the sheriff had to admit that it was not Red who killed Simon Gottman, that it was another member of his gang who had, himself, been killed by the famous Gunsmith.

So whom had Red killed? The answer was, no one, nor had he even ordered a killing. These were the lawyer's points.

Clint frowned. Red's lawyer was slick as cow slobber.

Hank scrubbed his jaw. "Used to be, a man was hung right on the spot for killing another, or for stealing his horse, or for using his woman. We all know Red Taggert is a killer and a thief, and it is a dead certain fact that he kidnapped and raped Mrs. Gottman."

The spectators swung around en masse to stare at Jane. Clint saw Jane's cheeks color slightly, but he also noted how her chin lifted a fraction. He was not sure the woman understood that she might have to go into some of the details of the kidnapping and rape, might have to go into a lot of the details if the judge were the kind of lecher and scum he appeared to be.

Judge Brennan turned to look at her and, for the first time, he seemed to show some interest in something besides fanning himself vigorously or swatting flies whenever one chanced to land within his reach.

"Mrs. Gottman," he said, clearing his throat with self-importance. "The sheriff admits that he has no direct proof that Red shot and killed your husband or ordered his death. To bring to bear the full penalties of the law of this territory, I and the jury will need to hear a full account of what went on after you and Red rode away."

Jane stood up and squared her shoulders. To Clint, she suddenly looked very soft and vulnerable, though he knew there was steel in her. She moved up to replace Hank Tilson at the witness stand. Hank looked bad; he had lost weight and there were dark circles under his eyes. It was hard to believe that he was still the only thing standing between order and lawlessness in this part of Arizona.

The judge swore Jane in and then told her to take a seat. The courtroom had suddenly become so still that you could hear a fly buzzing.

"Mrs. Gottman, in your own words, please tell us exactly what happened on the day you disappeared."

"I was kidnapped," she said tightly, "I did not just disappear. Red Taggert—that man sitting right in this courtroom—swept me off my feet and carried me away screaming."

"To where?"

"Into the desert," she said. "We fled at first, and then when it became apparent that there was going to be no pursuit, we slowed down and then stopped for the night."

The spectators, the jury, the judge, and the bailiff leaned forward with expectation.

"And then what happened?" the judge was finally forced to ask.

"Come morning, we rode on another ten miles or so and joined his gang."

The judge frowned with disappointment. "My dear woman," he said, "I am afraid that you will have to provide the court with a great deal more information."

"About what?"

Clint killed the urge to laugh outright. Jane knew very well what they all wanted to hear, and she was going to make this sleazy little judge come right out and ask for it, admit his own sick curiosity about all the sordid details of the rape. The question was: would Jane tell?

The judge fidgeted with some papers. His own cheeks reddened and he did not look at her when he cleared his throat and said, "About what he . . . ah . . . what Red did to you that night."

"He did the same that night as he did every night I was his captive." Jane took a keep and steadying breath. When she spoke, her voice was like desert sand. "He raped me."

The ladies in the audience gasped and began to fan themselves faster. The men swallowed and stared at Jane with lecherous eyes.

Judge Brennan blew his nose nervously and said, "That is a very serious charge. It needs closer examination. If you were indeed violated, then we need to be assured of the matter.''

Jane's face went brittle and her voice took on an edge. ''He pulled me out of the saddle, and we fell onto a dry riverbed where we fought. I scratched for his eyes and he grabbed me right here.'' She pointed to one of her breasts. ''He dug his fingers in and squeezed until I fainted. It hurt so terribly. When I opened my eyes a few minutes later, he had taken off all my clothes and was unbuttoning his pants.''

''Mrs. Gottman, I am not sure . . .'' The judge looked out at the spectators as if trying to read their minds. Expecting to see shock, he must have seen something else instead because he whispered, ''Please go on and spare us nothing of this ordeal.''

Jane's mouth twisted with contempt. ''He is huge, and when I saw the size of him and saw the animal passion in his eyes, I tried to fight once more, but it was too late. He plunged his staff deep into me and I cried out in pain. Then, to my horror, he began to yell over and over—''

Clint was on his feet. ''This is enough!'' he bellowed, grabbing Jane and pulling her out of the witness chair. ''Damn all of you! Who is on trial here anyway?''

''Order in the court!'' the judge cried, smacking his gavel down hard. ''Bailiff, escort that man out of this room!''

Clint held Jane on one arm and his other hand dropped to his gun. ''This whole thing is sick!'' he shouted, ''and I will be damned if I'll allow this to continue.''

''Bailiff!''

Clint drew his gun and aimed it right at the judge whose eyes widened with terror. ''This isn't a court of law. I am taking the accused and Mrs. Gottman to Phoenix where justice will be served.''

The judge stammered. ''You have no authority to do that! Bailiff! Sheriff! Someone arrest this man!''

The bailiff wasn't even worth Clint's notice, but Hank Tilson damn sure was. What it had come down to was whether Hank was willing to back him up and lose his job.

"Hank," Clint said. "This town isn't worth shaming a fine career. You know what was happening in this so-called trial and that nothing Jane would have said would have mattered when they came to reaching a verdict. Make up your own mind. Are you with me or against me?"

"I'm with you," the old lawman said without a moment's hesitation. "You take her and I'll bring Red along behind. There is a stage due to leave for Phoenix this afternoon and we can hole up in my jail until it arrives."

Clint visibly relaxed. He did not know what he would have done if his old friend had decided to sell out for security and a two-bit job as sheriff for a second-rate town filled with cowards.

He glanced at Red Taggert who had not said a word so far. But the man was watching and he was smiling. He looked anything but worried about his fate in Phoenix. And as Clint led Jane toward the door, he had a sinking feeling that he was playing right into the outlaw leader's hands.

Chapter Ten

"Here it comes," Hank said, pulling out his watch and checking it, "and she is right on time. We are in luck; only two stages come through a week."

Clint nodded. Just inside the door, Hank had stacked everything he had accumulated in a lifetime of being a lawman and all of it didn't fill two good canvas bags.

Outside, it was brutally hot, and as the stage rolled past, Clint saw that the horses were staggering with fatigue and wringing wet. The thermometer stood at 114 in the shade and was still inching upward.

Clint studied Jane and wondered at how a woman could keep looking fresh in this heat. Not only was the trip going to be hard on her, but just being forced to endure the company of Red Taggert in the same coach would be a trial. Clint had already decided that, if the man didn't keep his big mouth shut, he would keep him gagged all the way to Phoenix.

"What if there are other passengers who want to come along?" Hank asked.

"We discourage them," Clint said firmly. "This is going to be a dangerous trip and a tough one. Only a fool would invite himself along for the ride rather than wait for the next stage."

Hank nodded. He hoisted his bags and looked thoughtfully around the small jail and sheriff's office. "Isn't much, is it?" he muttered. "Worst office I ever been in charge of, but I think I'll still miss it some. I have had some good days in

Desert Springs, days when I was proud to wear the badge and keep law and order."

"Maybe you can find a better town," Clint said with a shrug of his broad shoulders. "Could be they need a good lawman in Phoenix."

"Uh-uh," Hank said. "All the jobs are going to the younger men nowadays. Nobody wants an old fart like me coming in all set in his ways and wanting to run the show like I been doing all my life."

Clint understood. When he had first gotten into being a lawman, there had been plenty of old-timers who were all too eager to give advice and criticize his inexperience. He had railed against them and, as often as not, found out he could have saved himself a lot of grief had he listened and learned from the earlier mistakes of older and wiser men. But the young ones in any profession always figure they know every damn thing—as if they were mysteriously born with some great wisdom. And they always wind up learning the hard way. But as lawmen, many never lived past the first few lessons.

Hank Tilson went and unlocked the cell and said, "Turn around and put your hands behind your back, Red."

The man did as he was ordered. "Don't lose the key to those handcuffs, sheriff. My boys will be needing it pretty quick."

Hank fastened the cuffs on tightly and stuffed the key in his shirt pocket. "You just button that lip of yours or I will take out a needle and stitch it shut."

"You'd do it, wouldn't you?" Red said with a sneer.

"Damn right, I would."

Clint picked up his own gear. He would tie Duke to the rear of the coach and let him come along behind. He hated to make the gelding travel through this heat, but at least this way, he would not have to carry any weight on his back.

"You ready, Jane?"

"Yes, whenever you are." She had several suitcases of things to take along. They had talked this over very carefully.

She knew that her testimony would be necessary in order to get a hanging verdict from a Phoenix judge and jury.

With Jane on the stand, and a court not afraid of reprisal, hanging would be virtually assured. After the conviction, it was her intent to return to this town, sell out, leave, and never come back. Jane had hard feelings about these people who had refused to help her or join the posse with her husband; Clint did not blame her at all.

He picked up the sheriff's Winchester rifle and took Jane's arm. "Let's get out of this hellhole."

"Won't be any cooler in Phoenix, Clint."

"Maybe not, but I guarantee that there are plenty more ways to enjoy yourself there."

She smiled. "Perhaps when this is all over, I mean when we have finished with the trial and I have sold everything off, then . . ."

"Hey!" Red crowed. "Don't you be offering him your charms and your money, Jane! Hell, save it for just the two of us. I'll show you a high old time in San Francisco. Why—"

Clint didn't wait to hear anymore. He drew his gun and stuffed the barrel into Red's open mouth. The meaning could not have been clearer and Red's eyeballs damn near crossed themselves staring down at that length of steel.

Clint slowly removed the gun. "Next time, it may go off by accident and that would be a damned messy shame, wouldn't it, Red?"

The man nodded vigorously and he did not speak.

They made quite a sight as they marched up to the coach. The stagecoach driver and his guard were no more pleased than the man who reluctantly sold them tickets. "I wish you would rent a carriage," the seller whined. "With Red Taggert, it is a pure invitation to disaster. My company—"

"Hang your company!" Clint growled.

"Well, I'm not going to get myself shot over this!" the guard yelled. "This two-bit stage don't pay me enough to die for it. I quit!"

"Good riddance," Hank growled. "Someone with no

more loyalty than that ought to be mucking out stalls instead of pretending to be a real man. I'll take his place. Clint, you ride in the coach with Red and Mrs. Gottman."

Clint nodded. "All right, but we can trade off every few hours. You are going to bake up there."

They both studied the driver and it was Clint who asked, "You going to quit, too?"

The man spit a stream of tobacco. He was small, wiry, and fierce with forearms as thick as tree branches and probably as hard. He wore a gray, sweat-stained hat and high boots. Stuffed behind his belt was a gun and a bowie knife. The driver looked as if he could whip his weight in teased tom-cats.

"It's my stage and no one is going to take it, not the Apache, not outlaws, and not you, Hank."

"All we want is a ride to Phoenix," Hank said respectfully. "Caleb, we paid the full fare; that makes us entitled to ride same as anyone else."

The driver thought. He spat again and said, "Ought to pay more if you bring us trouble, but we can talk that over in Phoenix."

"Fair enough," Hank said gravely. "But if trouble comes, I want you to know that this man down in the coach is the Gunsmith."

Caleb studied him up and down. "I know that," he said finally. "Saw you ten years ago in a gunfight. You still the best?"

"I don't know. But I can still usually hit what I aim for," Clint said quietly.

"Bet you can at that," Caleb said with a slow wink. He stuck out his hand to shake Clint's. It was like gripping a giant eagle's talon. It was strong and hard with calluses. "I am honored to have you ride my coach, Gunsmith. If I owned the company, I'd let you go for free."

"Thanks," Clint said, managing to disengage his hand without its receiving permanent damage.

The fresh horses were in harness. The day wasn't getting

any cooler. "All aboard," Caleb grunted.

Clint handed Hank his Winchester, tied Duke behind the stage, and gave Jane a hand up into the coach.

"So long everybody!" Red yelled to the spectators who had gathered to see his departure. "I'll be back to visit you real soon!"

"Get in!" Clint hissed, shoving the man forward. "You have speeches to make, make them on the gallows."

Red twisted to glare at him. "I'd make you a wager I never reach Phoenix, but it's hard to collect from a corpse. Lots of things can happen between here and there."

Clint shoved the man inside and followed. He sat next to Jane. "Let me tell you something, Red. If push comes to shove and there is no hope for me, I will kill you. Bet on that."

The outlaw managed a thin smile, but when he spoke, his voice was strained. "Well, Gunsmith, I reckon that means we are in for one hell of an interesting trip, doesn't it?"

Clint checked his gun. He absently pointed it at Red and then he cocked the hammer and watched the man press himself back into his seat with terror. He eased the hammer forward and holstered the weapon. "You had better pray that your friends have deserted you, Red."

The man expelled a deep breath. He was sweating heavily when he said, "I got nothing to lose getting a little help from my friends. Nothing at all."

Clint felt Jane's hand seeking his own. She gripped it tightly and he wished they were alone so that he could tell her to relax, that everything was going to be fine. But Jane was too smart for that. She knew as well as he did that Red had it pegged true—he did have nothing to lose in the event his gang tried to rescue him.

And that had Clint worried.

Chapter Eleven

There were men, and Clint had actually met a few, who thought the desert was beautiful. It always worried Clint when he heard someone say that because he just figured that they had suffered brain damage from frying in the sun. To Clint, this was the country that God forgot—either that, or he got tired and decided to brush over it real fast after doing his best work in the mountains and across the prairies.

Oh sure, the giant cactus were interesting to look at. They came in fascinating shapes and sizes, and with a little imagination, you could make them into all sorts of things. But the rest of the country—the dry, twisted hills and arroyos; the distances stretching into blurry haze; the flat washed-out skies—were tedious and offered nothing to him. Sometimes the coach passed by a coyote, and while these dogs of the hills usually lit out at the first sight of man, here they just seemed too damned listless to care. Clint wondered why anything that had the ability to leave the desert did not up and do it.

Traveling in the coach was a blessing compared to being up on top in the sun, but it was still no picnic. The heat was stifling; the air was choked with fine dust. Clint leaned his head back and tried to imagine they were in the mountains or out on the grassy prairies of Wyoming, Texas, or Montana. It did not work. He sat and sweated and knew that this trip was something that he would just have to endure.

"You know," Red said easily, "I can tell by looking at you that you are not a man who likes nor understands the desert."

Clint opened one eye. "And you are?"

Red nodded. "It suits me better than most. Especially at night—and the evenings and early mornings are pretty fine. Then, too, there ain't many men want to join a posse and chase me into the desert. You see, unless a man knows how to live like an Apache, unless he knows how to find the waterholes and how to travel across a desert, it'll rightly kill him."

"And you know all that?"

Red grinned. "Sure I do! I was raised by the Apache when I was a boy. I could travel across this desert on foot and come out fatter than when I started."

"Good for you," Clint said dryly.

"You don't believe me, do you?"

"I don't much care one way or the other."

"How about you, Jane? You believe me? You seen how I traveled across the desert."

"I believe you," she whispered. "But I don't care either."

Red chewed on that silently for about a minute. "How much you figure all your husband's property is worth?"

"Shut up," Clint warned, "or I'll gag you."

"How much?" he recklessly insisted.

Clint started to lean forward. He was in no mood for the man's impertinence.

"No," Jane said, throwing out an arm to restrain him. "That's all right. I don't mind answering his questions. My husband was worth probably twenty to thirty thousand dollars, though I doubt I'll get that much for everything."

"*Woowee!*" Red whistled. "That is a lot of money. I did not think the entire town of Desert Springs was worth that much!"

"It isn't to me," she told him.

"Ha! Or to me either!" He stopped smiling, glanced nervously at Clint, and then pushed on. "Jane, why don't you tell this man the truth about us, how you wanted me to take you away. Come on now!"

"That's a lie!" she said in a quavering voice.

"The hell it is!" he spat. "You and I had—"

Clint backhanded the man across the mouth, and when he hollered, Clint stuffed a handkerchief into his mouth and then used a second one to tie it in place. All the while, Red was coughing and his face was turning purple.

"He's choking to death!" Jane cried, starting to grab at the handkerchief.

Clint stopped her. "He'll live to hang. All he has to do is start breathing through his nose. See, he's looking better already. Why are you so worried about the man? He's not telling the truth, is he?"

"Of course not!" she said angrily. "But no one could sit idly by and watch another human choke to death without trying to help."

Clint shrugged. "He would kill me or Hank Tilson in a second without giving it a thought. Fact of it is, he would probably kill us slow if he had the opportunity. I don't have much sympathy for such a man."

"He once had a mother who loved him."

"What has that got to do with anything?"

Jane clamped her mouth shut and turned her face toward the window. Watching her, Clint wondered if Red was telling the truth and this pair had been secret lovers. If true, then it would mean that Jane Gottman was an accomplice to the murder of her husband. Clint did not believe for a moment that the girl had intended for her husband to be killed, but intended or not, that would not matter in a court of law.

I'll have to watch her, too, he thought, suddenly feeling a bit edgy. I'll just have to see what the hell is going to happen. And if we are attacked by Red's gang, then I guess that will be the moment of truth. Jane Gottman will just have to decide which one of us matters the most.

They rolled into a stage stop late that afternoon and changed horses. Clint watered Duke and stayed with Red until it was time to push on. Then he traded places with Hank.

The heat was starting to subside a little, but it was still well over a hundred degrees, and without any overhead covering, he felt as if he were frying.

Caleb was no talker. He chewed tobacco and spit at targets they passed. He was a remarkable spitter, one of the best Clint had ever seen. He could hit a rock at twenty feet as the coach careened over the rough road, and whenever he had a chance to drench a horned toad, he gave it his very best shot and then laughed with perverse delight.

Mile after blistering mile they traveled and the country did not change. When they reached the next stage stop, it was to stay for almost an hour to eat and rest. When Hank climbed up on the roof of the stage, Clint ushered the outlaw and the lady inside. They would travel all night and most of the next day and a half in order to reach Phoenix.

"Say," Red offered, "how about undoing these handcuffs and letting me get some circulation going in my hands?"

"Nope," Clint responded.

"Why not? I saw the sheriff give you the key. You can do it."

"Sure I can, but I won't. Only reason he gave me the key is in case this thing should tip over or something. Then I might need your hands. Caleb says we are entering some rough hills and deep canyons up ahead. The stage has been known to get stuck."

"If we tip over or get stuck, I'll be damned if I lift a finger to help. Wouldn't be very smart of me, would it?"

"Sure it would," Clint said easily. "Be smarter than giving me the excuse I need to shoot you between the eyes."

Red's face went ugly. "Hard to believe you were ever a man of the law. I bet you executed plenty of men rather than bother to see they got a fair trial."

"As a matter of fact, I have never executed anyone, but you would be a good one to start on. And if—"

His words were interrupted as the coach suddenly luched heavily sideways and Clint heard Caleb's whip crack like a shot. He looked out and saw that the stage was churning slowly through deep sand and despite everything that the horses could do, they were grinding to a standstill.

"Everybody out!" Clint ordered, "and let's give those horses some help or we are going to be here a long time digging the wheels free."

"The handcuffs?"

Clint swore to himself, but he produced the key. They were going to need every ounce of Red's considerable strength. "One mistake and you are dead," he warned.

Red nodded and smiled. "Sure enough, Gunsmith. I am a man who always obeys orders."

He was leering and on the verge of laughter and Clint wished he could belt him across his arrogant, smirking mouth, but he could not. "Come on, Jane. I'm afraid we're going to need your strength, too."

"All right."

They piled out into the dry riverbed and threw their shoulders to the wheel. Hank was down with them and, somehow, they got the wheels turning again as Caleb urged his team to a maximum pulling effort. "Don't ease up now!" he shouted. "Keep it up until we reach hard ground. We almost made it now."

Thirty feet from solid ground the first bullet ripped into the stage and it was closely followed by others.

"We are under attack!" Hank Tilson shouted, jumping up into the driver's seat and scrambling for his Winchester.

Red started to twist and run, but Clint hit him with a fist and knocked him back against the stage. "Damn you," he yelled, "keep pushing until we are out of this riverbed!"

And push they did, all three. With bullets hissing around them, they somehow managed to push on through the sand and get the stage back on solid ground. Clint grabbed Jane and almost threw her up and into the coach.

Red hesitated and Clint drew his gun and yelled, "Get in there or I kill you now!"

Red jumped for the door as the coach lurched forward. Clint grabbed the door. Suddenly he heard a cry and looked up to see Hank. The man had dropped his rifle and was hugging his chest with both hands, trying to stem a pulsing flow of blood. Then he toppled forward and no one had to tell Clint that the old lawman was dead.

"Roll her!" Clint bellowed as he jumped to take Hank's place. Without cover, Caleb wouldn't last fifteen seconds, and now, as the team began to run, Clint grabbed his old friend's rifle and raised it.

There were at least fifteen riders—all of them armed and firing as they seemed to fly across the sandy riverbed and take up the chase. Clint knew that Red was free down below, but there was nothing he could do to help Jane Gottman. If he managed to stand off the gang, he would take care of Red when the stage slowed, and if they were overtaken by the outlaws, none of it mattered anyway.

Caleb was shouting and using his whip, and the team, though already exhausted and winded from its efforts to pull the coach from the clinging sand, gave its best.

But the gang was closing fast. Clint shot three out of the saddle and was taking aim on a fourth when a bullet creased his side and knocked his aim off. He lifted the rifle with bloody hands and then he heard a soft groan. He twisted around too late. He tried to grab the driver before Caleb pitched out onto the desert floor and rolled to a stop against a cactus.

Clint stared down at the dragging reins. Then he looked ahead as the road swung sharply around a ridge and past a steep drop down into a canyon.

My God, he thought, we'll never make the turn! The coach is going to fly over the side. We've got to jump!

But he just couldn't do it—not with Jane riding below and probably fighting for her life. Clint dropped the Winchester and reached for the brake. He had to slow the stagecoach. And if they shot him while he was trying to do that, well, maybe he could save the woman from being thrown over the cliff to a certain death.

His hands wrapped around the long wooden handle and he

leaned back with all his might. There was a terrible screech-ing sound, followed instantly by smoke. As the coach began to slow just a little, rider loomed up beside him and fired almost point-blank.

The Gunsmith went up on his toes and his vision turned into a sheet of blood. He felt himself falling, and then he felt nothing at all.

Chapter Twelve

Jane Gottman had never been so terrified in her entire life. The coach was bouncing over rocks and moving wildly from one side to the other and was obviously out of control. That meant that everyone on top was dead and that the coach was going to crash and she would probably die. And even if, by some miracle, she survived, she would be at the mercy of Red Taggert once again. If given the choice of being a captive or of dying, she would choose being captive.

"What are you going to do?" she cried.

Red stuck his head out the window and didn't look a bit concerned until he saw the drop just ahead and realized that they would not make the curve.

"Jesus!" he shouted, throwing open the door and studying the ground as it whipped past. "We're gonna wreck. We got to jump!"

But try as she might, Jane just could not make herself do that. The ground was flying past at such horrifying speed she was certain that she would break her neck or spine if she hurled herself out the door. "There must be a better way!"

Red had to be thinking along a similar line because he nodded. "I think I can get a leg over the Gunsmith's horse that's tied behind. If I do, I'll ride up and grab for you, Jane. That's the best I can do!"

"Then hurry!"

Red nodded. "Wait until I get my hands on those stupid sonsofbitches. Some rescue!"

He slammed the door open and managed to throw himself

in the rear boot. Jane could not see him, but with her head craned out the door, she knew that he had not fallen or she would have seen his body on the rutted road.

She twisted around and her hand flew to her mouth—the sharp curve was less than a hundred yards ahead! She steeled herself for what she knew she must do to have any chance of survival. She would jump. And just when she rocked forward out of her seat and was ready to leap, Red Taggert suddenly thundered up beside her on Duke's back.

"Come on!" he bellowed, reaching out for her. "Jump!"

She took a deep breath and leaped for him, arms flailing wildly. And then, miraculously, he had her and was reining in the horse as the rest of the outlaw gang overtook them.

One man swept past in a valiant attempt to grab the lead horse, but he failed. When the stage hit the curve and broke free, Jane screamed to see the four horses lift up into the air and go spinning away over the cliff.

"Shit!" Red whispered, shaking his head. "Damn, but I hate to see horses go that way."

He reined Duke to a walk, and when the rest of his gang came to circle him, he bellowed, "You dumb bastards almost got us killed! What the hell is wrong with your brains? Couldn't you find a better place to jump the stage?" No one answered and after Red glowered at them for a few minutes, he grunted, "Everyone dead?"

"Yeah," a blocky man in his thirties with a yellow shirt answered.

"The Gunsmith, too?"

"Dead certain. Jess plugged him in the belly, and then I got him in the head. He dropped like a stone and we rode right over the top of what was left of him."

"Good."

Red squeezed Jane hard and she snapped, "Quit it!"

"What's the matter, honey? You feel bad about the Gunsmith? He knew what kind of trouble he was buying into. Me, I feel pretty damned good—got me my pretty woman back and got the finest horse in Arizona."

"I'll never be your woman!" She wanted to scratch away his leering face.

He laughed out loud and so did his men. "You'll be mine or theirs," he said. "Take your pick."

She shivered despite the heat, and when he unbuttoned her blouse and stuck his hand inside to fondle her breasts, she let him.

"What about the stage?" an outlaw asked.

Red traced a finger around and around her nipple. "You boys ride down there and put the team out of its misery, any that might still be alive. Then gather up anything worth keeping and wait for me."

"What are you . . .?"

Red winked and they all chuckled. Jane felt herself being pulled off the horse. "Damn you," she said when he dropped her to the dirt. "You are nothing but an animal, Red Taggert."

He stood over her, a tall, beautifully proportioned man with red hair and a full erection poking at his pants as he began to unbuckle his belt.

"I hate you!"

"Then fight me, woman. That'll just make it all the more fun. But remember this before you try to rake out my eyes: I am the man who just saved your pretty neck."

He dropped his pants and smiled. "Now, how do you want it, rough or easy?"

Jane Gottman swallowed as she stared at him and felt the heat rising within her and was ashamed because of it. When he realized the effect he was having on her, he roared with delight.

She averted her eyes and began to undress.

Chapter Thirteen

Clint awoke slowly, reluctantly. There was a buzzing in his head and he hurt all over. He tried to go back to sleep, but the buzzing sound was growing too loud. He groaned, opened his eyes, and found himself staring at a coiled rattlesnake.

Suddenly, all thought of drifting back into unconsciousness vanished and his body tensed. The rattler was huge, as big around as his wrist, and it must have been six feet long. It was down near his feet and Clint forced himself to think. Was he wearing his gun? If so, did it have any bullets left in the chamber? He wasn't sure. There was such a violent pounding in his skull that it seemed as if his thoughts were disintegrating as fast as he could form them. He eased his hand along behind his back, down toward his waist, and out of sight of the rattler—or so he thought. The snake began to buzz even faster.

He broke out in a cold sweat, even though the temperature was blistering his flesh. His fingers nudged his gun and he tried to pull the weapon free, but there was too much weight on it. He knew that any movement at all would invite the rattler to strike.

What do I do now? he thought desperately.

He waited. Sweat coursed down his forehead and into his eyes. They stung. He had lost his Stetson and the sun made his head throb and pound faster and faster until his vision began to blur. He tried to swallow and could not. His side ached. Still, the snake remained coiled in the shade of a bush and watched him, its forked tongue darting out every so often as if to taunt him into making a fatal move.

Clint closed his eyes for a moment and tried to think, one careful word at a time. If I move, I will be struck. If I do not move, I will pass out and the snake will be able to hit me nearer the heart where its poison will work faster. I must move.

He filled his lungs over and over, trying to keep his chest from rising or falling but wanted the air to clear his mind. He would move because he had to and the snake would strike. That much was certain. What was not certain was if he could get his boot into the reptile's face and deflect the fangs long enough to roll and come up firing.

Clint wiggled his fingers to make sure they were functioning, and then, tensing, he studied the distance between one boot and the snake. It was going to be hairy, no question about it.

Now! He kicked out at the creature and it struck so fast that it was just a blur. He felt its fangs grab the heavy leather uppers of his boots. But at the same time, he was rolling sideways and his gun was jumping out of its holster and coming alive in his hand. He kicked again and the snake reared back and began to strike again, higher this time, up where there was only denim.

There was no time to aim, no time to think. All he could do was react with swiftness and that is exactly what the Gunsmith did as his first bullet entered the gaping mouth, passed cleanly between the spaced fangs, and blew the rattler's brain out of the back of its sinister little head.

Clint sagged with relief. He pushed himself up on his haunches, and the world tilted crazily for a moment and then righted itself as he went to his knees. He shielded his eyes with the palm of one hand while he absently holstered his gun. The buzzing sound was gone and in its place lay a terrible silence. There was no wind, not even a faint breeze, and the country in which he now found himself stranded lay suffering and silent.

Clint traced the wheel marks on the desert floor. His eyes followed them from the west to the east and then he stood up swaying with unsteadiness. Which direction should he go? To return to the west might be the smartest, for he remembered there was a stage station some thirty miles back. He was not certain that he could walk that far. He had lost blood; his side was caked with it from the flesh wound along his ribs and the left side of his head was matted with hair and blood.

Clint looked to the west a long, long time before he decided he had not the strength to make it thirty miles with nothing in between. Unhurt and with water, yes. Weak and without water, no chance at all. He turned to the east and took a halting step forward, then another. His legs felt rubbery, his knees weak. But maybe he would grow stronger if he were able to find water. Red Taggert had bragged that he knew how to think and survive in this country.

Clint tried hard to work up a glob of spit and moisten his lips. I'm no damned Apache, he thought, and I haven't a chance in hell of finding water out here. So I'll follow these tracks until I find either the coach or Red and his outlaws. I might yet get out of this alive.

He stood at the top of a hill gazing down at the smashed coach, the dead horses, and the body of Hank Tilson. Clint felt his insides flood with a fiery anger that threatened to choke off his breath. Up in the sky, buzzards had appeared, and though he did not know where they might have come from, he knew that they had some instinctual sense of death and disaster. There was only one blessing to this, and that was that his own horse, Duke, was not lying broken at the base of the hill along with the team of horses.

Clint started down the side of the drop, wondering if he would have the strength to come back out when he was finished burying Hank Tilson. It did not matter. You did not leave a man like that to have his bones picked clean by scavengers. Besides, perhaps there were other bodies inside the wreckage, those of Jane Gottman and Red Taggert.

A half hour later he knew that the outlaw and the woman had escaped. Somehow, he did not find this surprising. It seemed clear to him that, given the choice between going over the side and leaping from the coach, anyone would leap. Clint crawled inside what was left of the interior of the coach. It was quite collapsed and he had to wriggle through a window. He was looking for a canteen that might have been overlooked by the outlaws. More than anything in the world, he needed water.

Caleb had always carried a barrel of water just for emergencies, but it was smashed and the water had long since drained into the desert floor. There was not enough moisture left to dampen a rag. No, if there was water to be found, it had to be inside the wreckage.

He tried to quell his rising anxiety as he poked through the wreckage, sorted through his own gear and that of Hank Tilson. Much of it had been looted, things of value probably distributed among the outlaw band. Clint mopped the sweat from his forehead and kept picking through the rubble. Not until he had almost given up did he find the cheap, tin flask almost filled with bad whiskey.

The whiskey was hot, and when he poured a tiny rivulet of its contents down his parched gullet, he choked from its raw fire. The whiskey came up through his nose and it burned. His eyes ran with tears and it was several minutes before he tried to drink again. This time he sipped the liquor even more slowly.

It made beads of sweat erupt from his forehead and he cursed his luck for not finding water instead. But he did not curse with any sincerity, for he understood that the whiskey might just save his life if he rationed it over a few days. It might just be enough to get him to the next stage station or desert spring or to someone who carried water.

Clint thought he ought to get out of the stagecoach and bury Hank now, but he felt too weak. He needed to eat and he had no food. He eyed the dead horses with distaste for a long time before forcing himself to climb out and carve a haunch of meat from the nearest one's hindquarter.

He had matches and he used shattered wood from the coach to build a fire. The sun was just going down when he finished eating. He kept telling himself that, to the Apache, the horse was better eating than cattle or sheep. But he wasn't a damned Apache. The meat was rank and tough as rawhide. Still, he knew that he had to keep up his strength.

Clint had to beat off a swarm of black flies to cut more strips of meat from the horse, and when he had an even dozen, he laid them over sticks and let them sizzle and smoke until they grew black and curled up with the heat. Jerky. He had never appreciated beef jerky; he wondered how he would manage to swallow this type of jerky.

Finished, he now faced the most disagreeable task of all, that of taking care of his old lawman friend. Clint knew that he did not have the strength necessary to dig a grave or even to gather rocks and cover Hank enough to keep the coyotes from burrowing to his body. He did the only decent thing he could think of. He dragged Hank over and stuffed him into the wrecked coach. Then he set fire to the whole works.

He stepped back, a blood-caked, gaunt, and haggard man. The fire gushed greedily from the coach's windows and split seams. He held the lawman's badge up to the red glow of the flames. It read: Sheriff—Desert Springs, Arizona.

Clint's lip curled with contempt and he hurled the badge into the flaming coach. The outlaws had even stolen Hank's gun, but they had not bothered to unbuckle his worn gunbelt.

Clint punched the bullets out of the gunbelt and dropped them into his pocket. When he found Red Taggert and his men, he would need plenty of bullets. He was going to kill every one of those bastards.

Close by, a coyote howled. There were four dead horses left for it and the black buzzards to eat.

The Gunsmith turned and studied the slope back up to the road. He filled his lungs with air and then he attacked the slope, clawing and fighting and snarling. He grabbed and ripped and tore at the brush until he finally threw his body onto the road where he lay gasping.

Then, when he was able, he stood on trembling legs and

stared down at the fire and the coyotes, which already had moved in on the dead horses.

Death and only death waited here. Clint started east one step at a time. This desert wasn't going to kill him, and neither would Red Taggert whenever he finally overtook the man.

He had a score to settle and a woman to free.

Chapter Fourteen

He was moving very slowly down the road, wishing that it would cool off. Overhead, the stars were brilliant, but down on the desert floor there was nothing but heat and pain. Clint studied the stars and determined it to be around three in the morning. He decided that he could allow himself another sip of the whiskey, but the very thought of it made him grimace. Life was funny: When you had water, you yearned for something like whiskey, but when whiskey was all you had to slake a thirst, it was a damn poor substitute for water.

Clint was bone weary, moving without thought, one step at a time. His mind needed something to grasp hold of in order to keep him from worrying about what a mess he was in right now. His body halted. There was a fork in the road.

"Well, I'll be damned," he muttered, sipping the whiskey and grimacing. It seemed amazing to Clint that the road would fork right out here in the middle of nowhere. But it did. The rutted stagecoach trail angled off to the left and a small horse trail went to the right. Clint studied it carefully. It was obvious that Red Taggert and his boys had taken the horse trail.

Clint took a deep breath and swayed with fatigue. The amount of blood he had lost had weakened him considerably and he was so exhausted that he had to concentrate on the decision that faced him squarely.

If he trudged along the horse trail and tried to overtake Red, he probably would fail, and he would drop and die in the desert and never be found. But, Clint thought, turning to the

77

stagecoach road, if I go this way, I may lose the outlaw trail and that I do not want.

Clint took one more tiny sip of whiskey to clear the fog of fatigue from his brain. It seemed like a simple decision of left or right, but he knew the wrong decision would cost him his life.

He chose to follow the stage road. There just had to be a stage station out here somewhere and there he would find water. He had about a hundred dollars in his jeans and that would buy him water and canteens, a rifle, and a damn good horse, one able to catch up with the Taggert gang. And when he did, he would even the score. He would show no mercy to Red and he would rescue Jane Gottman.

Just thinking about that made Clint's chin lift a little and his stride quicken. Somewhere soon, there had to be a stage station.

Dawn came way too early on the desert.

First, there was a faint light to the east, then a gradual transformation of black to silver-gray, and then the clouds became tinged with salmon. Entire columns of hills, heavily armed cactus, and huge outcroppings of rock all seemed to appear magically from out of nothing. And the moment the sun reared its brilliant, flaming head over the eastern edge of the world, the temperature soared.

Clint studied a low line of hills up ahead where the road he followed sliced over their top and disappeared. One more line of sun-baked hills to climb, one more sweltering valley beyond to cross, one more . . .

He stopped. The heat was already intense enough to create mirages, big shimmering lakes of water, but this was different. A spot of green that appeared to be an honest-to-God tree and . . . yes! a —house dug out of the hills about two miles to the left of the stage road.

Clint swallowed. He squinted so hard his eyes watered. Was this the first sign of his mind cracking? Or were the tree and the house for real?

Clint started walking again. Faster. If that was a house and that was a tree, then there had to be water. But if not, then he was going to know that his mind was starting to unravel, that the heat, the loss of blood and the whiskey were all combining to rob him of his senses.

"Be real!" he said in a cracked voice. "Be real!"

Chapter Fifteen

"That's far enough!" a voice boomed. "Just you turn it around and head on back down that road before I put a bullet through you."

Clint stopped dead in his tracks. He was covered with sweat, his chest was heaving in and out, and all he could do was stare at the green tree and marvel at its beauty.

"You hear me or are your brains fried and sizzled clean away?"

He tore his eyes from the tree and tried to focus on the cabin before him. Whoever was inside wasn't showing himself, only the barrel of his buffalo gun, a gun that could blow a hole through you as big around as a coffee can.

Clint tried to raise his arms away from the gun at his side, but the effort was too great; his arms felt like they each weighed a hundred pounds. He tried to speak, but his voice was nothing but a tortured whisper.

"You look in awful bad shape. I don't need none of your trouble, got enough here of my own."

Clint took a step forward and the buffalo rifle lifted. He heard it cock menacingly. Then the man inside the house yelled, "Go on, now! Get away before I do you a favor and put you out of your misery!"

Clint had finally managed to work up enough spittle to moisten the inside of his mouth. He knew two things, the first being that he wasn't going to leave without some water, and the second was that a man who asked you twice to leave wasn't the kind who would shoot you down in cold blood.

"Water . . ." Louder and stronger now. "Water! I need a drink!"

The rifle dipped a little. "Oh, well, water is hard to come by in this country as you might have discovered. I didn't come by it free and I don't give water away to anybody. Water will cost you ten dollars a cup."

Clint stood shaking with helpless anger and fatigue. He was being robbed, but he would have paid every cent he had for a cup of water and not complained. He nodded.

"Let me see the color of your money."

"Let me see the water," Clint croaked.

The rifle barrel vanished and a moment later, a grizzled old prospector appeared in the doorway. He was as strange a looking bird as Clint had ever seen, but never had a man with a tin cup of water been a more revered sight. The prospector had an old Colt pistol cocked in his big fist and he approached slowly. He was a giant; he wore moccasins and a Mexican serape that draped only as far as his crotch. He might have been sixty years old but could easily have been eighty. His hair and his beard were white except for around his mouth where the hair was stained yellow and brown from chewing tobacco.

"Your ten dollars!"

Clint dug it out of his pocket, never taking his eyes off the old man who, though he moved with a slight limp and was a little bent, still cast a mighty long shadow across the dirt. The gun in his fist looked like a kid's toy.

They made the exchange, money for water, and Clint could not keep his hand from shaking and spilling some of the water. It took all of his resolve not to drink it down in a single gulp; something warned him his stomach, so long deprived of water, would revolt and he'd retch and lose it all. So he sipped slowly and stared at the man who towered over him.

"You going to want to buy a second cup of it?"

"Yeah," he answered, feeling stronger almost the instant he swallowed the first mouthful. "I want to trade whiskey for water."

The giant's eyes widened. "You got whiskey?"

Clint dared to allow one of his hands to leave the tin cup and drop to his back pocket where it located the flask, which was still almost half full.

The man's paw jerked toward the flask, but Clint pulled it back. "Whiskey for a full canteen and another cup of water."

"Ha!"

Clint slipped the flask back into his pocket. He pointed up at the big, spreading cottonwood. "If you can afford water to keep that growing, you can afford to make the trade."

The prospector closed one eye, and the other slitted. "There ain't nothing wrong with your brain yet. Good whiskey?"

Clint would not lie. "Poison?"

The giant swallowed. "All whiskey is good. You got a deal."

The man started to reach for the flask, but Clint stepped back. "First a canteen full and another cup. Then you can have it."

"You are a suspicious sonofabitch, ain't you?"

"Just cautious is all."

"I could have shot you, taken the whiskey, and kept my water."

"Yeah, you could have. But I could kill you right now and have all the water I want. So we are even."

"How do you figure that? I am the one holding the gun," he said, waving it up in Clint's face.

Clint drew his pistol and jammed it into the man's gut so fast that the prospector was caught totally by surprise. He stiffened, his own weapon still raised to the sky and of no help whatsoever.

Their eyes locked. Clint smiled and then put his gun away. "Go get the water and let's quit playing games. You are no killer and neither am I."

The giant nodded, waited until Clint had emptied the cup, and then went to get more.

A few minutes later, they settled under the shade of the cottonwood tree, and although the air was still hot, it seemed to Clint as if he had died and gone straight to heaven.

The prospector's name was Boris and he had been born in Poland and had come to this country with his parents around the turn of the century. Both his mother and father had slaved in the factories back east, working night and day until they had dropped dead on the job. Boris had actually walked over the Allegheny Mountains and swam the Mississippi River. Clint figured he was probably man enough to do that.

"So what are you doing out here in this hell?"

"Living," he answered simply.

"On what?"

"I find a little gold—not enough that anyone would want to risk trying to rob me. I hunt rabbits and birds."

"With a buffalo rifle?" Clint grinned. "You would blow them to pieces." The man did look awfully thin.

Boris nodded. "I need a new rifle," he admitted. "Are you a lawman?"

"No." Clint shook his head. "I used to be a lawman, but I am not one of those anymore. Right now, I am just a very desperate man on the trail of a gang of murderers."

"Who are they?"

"A man named Red Taggert and—what's the matter?"

The giant's face had transformed into one of hatred. "He took away my daughter. I wait for him to ride past here again so that I can shoot him with the buffalo rifle. And when I do, I'll blow a hole through his belly so that it will take him time to die. And while he is dying, I will take my knife and castrate him!"

Boris actually yanked a saber-size knife out of its leather sheath and hacked at the air. Watching, Clint could only pity Red if he ever came within striking distance of the huge Polish prospector. "The man killed a good friend of mine. His name was Sheriff Hank Tilson."

"Never heard of him," Boris said. "I don't like outlaws, and I don't like lawmen either. They are both out to steal what belongs to honest men; the lawman, he just chooses to do it legally.''

"That's an interesting way to look at it," Clint said, not wanting to argue the matter.

"Truth!"

"Maybe not," Clint said stubbornly. "Hank was honest to the core. When he left Desert Springs, everything he owned was in two canvas bags. He sure never cheated anyone."

"Then he was a dumb lawman." Boris poured whiskey down his throat and gritted huge yellow teeth and shuddered. "Red Taggert is mine to kill, not yours."

"I'd say that depends on which of us gets to him first." Clint stood up. "I can see you have nothing to ride, so I'd be grateful for directions to the nearest horse for sale."

"None around here. Not for fifty miles."

"How much farther down that road is the next stage station?"

He waved a big hand. "Just yonder, behind that ridge, another five miles. But they can't sell you any of their horses. They all belong to their company."

"I've got to have a horse!" Clint had not meant to yell but every hour that he delayed would mean the trail would grow fainter and the outlaws would have Jane Gottman another night.

"To go after Taggert?"

"That's right."

Boris finished the whiskey. "I can't let you kill him first," he said tightly. "Guess I will have to come along with you and shoot him."

Clint took in a deep breath. "We may never catch him on foot."

"You may be right," Boris said, "but we just might on a pair of good Missouri mules."

Clint's head snapped up. All the fatigue and weakness in his knees vanished. "Mules? You know where we can find us mules?"

Boris grinned; all his upper teeth were missing. "I keep a

pair inside the house so that they don't fall into the hands of the Apache who cotton to mule meat.''

A slow smile crossed Clint's mouth. "Boris," he said, pushing out his hand, "you got a deal. If we catch Red Taggert, you get the first shot at him with that cannon of yours—just as long as I get the second. Deal?''

"Deal.''

So they shook on it and then headed up to the cabin to bridle the Missouri mules. Riding a mule bareback was a far cry and a big step down from riding Duke, but mules were tough, like this land. And besides, with big Boris and his buffalo rifle, if they got within a mile of Red Taggert, the man was going to get ventilated.

For the first time since the stage had been ambushed, Clint knew real hope.

Chapter Sixteen

The mules were a little on the thin side, but tall and rangy. They were seal-brown. Each had a black stripe down its narrow back. They had white muzzles. When Clint tried to bridle the one he was supposed to ride, the damn thing clamped its teeth together. He had hell to pay trying to jam the bit into its mouth.

"Use your gun," Boris snorted.

"My gun?"

"Yep. Jam it in there and pry his mouth open."

"Uh-uh," Clint said with a shake of his head. "This gun of mine is going to need to shoot straight when we catch up with Taggert and his men."

"Suit yourself." Boris walked over to the mule, reared back, and bashed his huge fist into the side of the animal's mouth. The mule staggered, bellowed, and then parted its big yellow teeth that had snapped like a bear trap. That's when Boris jammed the cold steel bit between its teeth saying, "You got to be damned fast, Gunsmith, or you'll be missing fingers."

Clint nodded. He was having some real second thoughts about these mules. Outside, he could see the faded, heat-ravaged hills undulating into infinity. The thought of walking over them was even more intimidating than riding this mule.

"What's his name?"

"Sneezer. Mine is named Jug."

"Odd names."

"Sneezer sneezes a lot. Jug once drank a whole jug of my

whiskey and walked right into a cactus. Was pretty messy-faced for a while."

Clint said he guessed Jug must have been drunk and then dropped it at that. Boris was not a man who owned much and he traveled very light—just a sack of crumbling biscuits, some pretty gamy rabbit jerky, a couple of canteens, and two or three old newspapers he proudly announced he knew by heart.

"If you know them by heart, why read them anymore?" Clint asked.

"Just to test myself is all. When I can't recite them word for word anymore, I'll know that my brain has started to stewing and that I am finally ready for another whirl at marriage. I'll hunt me up some widow who can prospect ore, cook, shoot, and tan rabbit hides. Course, she'll also have to be a woman of means as well as be young and good-lookin'."

"Of course. Are we ready to go now?"

Boris squinted outside. "Soon as the sun touches the hills and the temperature starts to fall a mite, then we ride."

"But . . . well, hell," Clint complained, "Red Taggert and his men already have a big headstart."

"You don't know the desert, do you? Only a fool travels when the temperature is above one hundred and the sun is high. Taggert ain't no fool, and I supposed you weren't either. Besides, we take Sneezer and Jug out right now, they are liable to buck us off in a cactus and run away. If they did, I wouldn't blame them."

Clint bit off a grumble. What he wanted most, now that he had had a good long drink of fresh water, was to catch Red, free Jane Gottman, and then to see that the outlaw and his band were brought to justice.

"Patience." Boris yawned and walked to a mattress lying on the floor and stretched out for a nap. "If you don't learn patience, this desert will kill you for damn sure. Don't get yourself into a lather. It's a long, hard trail we are fixing to take."

"Do you have any idea where Red and his men go to hide?"

"Nope. But there are places out in this desert where there are grass, trees, and lots of water."

"Why aren't you living at one of them?"

"There are about ten good reasons," Boris said with great patience. "First, whenever you find good grassy country, you find a lot of people wanting it for themselves. Second, easy living makes a man and his mules soft and weak. Third, you can bet the Apache know about them and come 'round regular as ticks in the spring. Fourth, there usually ain't no gold under grass. Fifth—"

"Never mind," Clint said with exasperation. "Take your nap and I'll wake you when the sun goes down."

"You can do that, but I'd wake anyway. It's like . . . well, like I got a clock in my head and it is ticking away so that I always know when to wake up, when to feed the mules, when to take a leak, and when to—"

"Spare me," Clint groaned, heading for the outdoors and the shade of the tree.

He was not sure if he could stand Boris for however long it was going to take to track down the outlaws. Obviously, the man was dying to talk about anything that came into his head, except for what he knew and felt about Red Taggert. That, and that alone, it seemed, was just too painful. Clint wondered how and why Red had taken his daughter and what had become of her, if she were dead, if she were still with the outlaw band.

Clint figured he would find out the answers to these questions, but when it was time to trade bullets, he had to know if Boris was going to go to pieces or stay cool and be of some help in a showdown—the answer could spell the difference between rescuing Jane Gottman and needlessly getting himself and the woman killed.

Clint squatted and leaned his back up against the tree. He gazed out at the desert and decided that if he never saw it or anything like it again that was all right with him. Leave it for the coyotes, lizards, buzzards, and rattlers. Trouble was, like it or not, he was going to have to face it for a good while longer.

Chapter Seventeen

When sundown came, Boris was up and moving toward Jug. He tied his traveling things to the mule and said, "Reckon it is time we hit the trail."

"The trail to where?" Clint asked. "How do we know where to start?"

"Well, we could track to that burned stage, but that would be out of the way. My choice would be to angle to the northeast, up into the Gila Bend Mountains. If Taggert has a secret place, that's where it has to be."

"It's Apache country, isn't it?"

"All of the southern part of Arizona is Apache country," Boris said. "We just have to keep our eyes and ears ready for anything. Apaches can travel on foot so quiet and secretlike that you never see them until it's too late. Most Indians are fancy; they wear feathers and jewelry, like pretty trinkets and things, but not the Apache. He don't care about nothing but his stomach being full, killing, and not getting killed. He travels light and fast, he is tough and dirty, he will ride a horse or mule until it is run to death, and then he will climb off the poor critter and roast it for his supper. My wife was Apache."

"She must have been an exception," Clint said, not sure what to say after Boris' grim earlier assessment of the Apache.

"She was. Her father was a chief and she had some status among her people; otherwise, they'd have killed me the first time I showed up in their camp. My wife was good and real

91

tough. My daughter, her beauty gets from her mother. Tall, pretty, black hair, and brown eyes. A gem.''

Clint said, ''Why did Red Taggert take her away?''

''He didn't.'' In the moonlight Boris scowled. Huge, craggy, and fierce, Boris was also very troubled. ''That's why I never killed Taggert before. Maria went with him on her own. She said she loved the sonofabitch. She begged me not to come after her.''

''They why go now?''

Boris spat tobacco juice. ''Because of the Gottman woman you described. It means Taggert has a new woman. He must have either sold Maria to the Mexicans or another tribe of Apache or else he gave her to one of his men. Whatever he did, I'll kill him for it.''

Clint chewed on that for several hours. He kept turning over the idea that maybe Jane Gottman was Taggert's woman. But if that were true, then why would she have been willing to travel all the way to Phoenix and testify against the man? There was only one possible explanation to that and it was that Jane Gottman had known the stage would never reach Phoenix.

Riding the mule across the sweltering desert, Clint wished that he had never come to this part of the country. He wanted Duke back in the worst way and then he wanted to even the score with Taggert for killing Hank Tilson.

He was still thinking about that at three in the morning when suddenly Sneezer stopped dead in his tracks and his long ears shot forward. Boris raised a hand in warning.

Boris slid off his mule and quickly led it into a draw. Clint knew better than to ask more questions. He got off Sneezer. Now he heard an owl's hooting, only it carried a little longer than any owl he had ever heard.

''Apache.'' Hank whispered into his ear. ''A bunch of them and they're close.''

''They see us?'' Clint could feel the hair rise on the back of his neck. Any westerner would tell you that the Apaches were the most feared tribe, the toughest to kill, and the quickest to strike a deadly blow, especially in their own desert stronghold.

Boris listened. Anyone could tell that the hoots were getting closer. He drew his gun and Boris raised his buffalo rifle. Sneezer began to wheeze and Hank quickly clamped a powerful hand over the mule's muzzle. "They are coming," he said.

"Any chance of talking to them?"

"Nope. They'll want to eat the mules right here—while they torture us slow."

"I thought you were their friend? After all, you married one."

"A Tonto Apache. These are probably Chiricahua and they are a whole different crowd."

"You speak their language?"

Boris shook his rifle. "This is the only language they understand when they want something you have. Gunsmith, I hope you are as good as your reputation."

Clint took a deep breath. He had never expected to lose his life out in some godforsaken desert. Like everyone else, he had heard the horror stories of what the Apache were capable of doing to their prisoners before finally killing them: castration, mutilation, cactus spines thrust into a man's private parts. The stories were true, and Clint knew that, come hell or high water, he was not going to be taken alive.

"They are moving in close," Boris whispered, putting his back to Clint's and pulling his mule close.

"How many?"

"Damned if I know. But you can bet we'll soon find out."

Clint nodded. Sweat was beading on his brow and he wiped it off. He had a bad feeling things were going to be getting a lot hotter during the next few minutes.

Chapter Eighteen

It was chilling to wait, standing back to back, with a man who could only fire one bullet. Clint knew damn well there would be no time for Boris to reload the big, old rifle and get off a second shot. That meant that Clint would have to do most of the work.

Boris did have a huge knife in his belt. He had no doubts that the giant knew how to use it well. The Apache might have old rifles, and even if not, they had bows and arrows that were swift and deadly.

"No matter what happens," Boris said in a soft, rumbling voice, "we stay back to back. If we get separated, then neither of us will stand a chance. You got a knife?"

"A pocketknife."

"Shit," Boris said with disgust. "Lot of good that will do us."

"About as much good as that one-bullet relic you have."

He could feel Boris stiffen. "Here they come. Stay low with your eyes right at the level of Sneezer's backbone. And don't you disappoint me, Gunsmith."

"I'll do my level best," he promised.

And then, out of the blackness, an arrow hissed and Clint felt Sneezer stagger and bawl with pain. He saw a shadowy figure and he snapped off a bullet that split the night like a cleaver. The Apache screamed and then all hell broke loose.

They seemed to spring from the ground like ghosts out of a cemetery. They came fast and hard. The air was filled with arrows and Clint could hear the mules screaming as shafts buried themselves in their flesh. Sneezer was buckling at the knees and Clint dropped behind him, firing until his gun was empty and making every shot count.

He reloaded, his hands controlled and moving with practiced precision. Boris' rifle sounded like a cannon's roar when it exploded and, for a moment, the draw that they were in was blanketed with smoke.

The smoke saved his life. Two Apaches leaped over the dying mule and would have stabbed him, but Clint rolled sideways and in the smoke was momentarily unseen. He finished loading and snapped off two shots as the smoke cleared. Both Apaches died on the spot.

They were coming in from every direction and Clint drilled one each with his next four bullets.

He heard Boris gasp with pain and then turned to see that two Indians had knocked him off his feet and straddled his chest. One was hacking away at his scalp and the other was pulling his knife out of the giant's chest.

The Gunsmith went crazy. His own weapon was empty again and now there was no time to reload. He had no idea how many Apaches were left as he snatched up the heavy buffalo rifle by its barrel and began to club the pair. He crushed their skulls as if they were eggs, and then he twisted around and took on two more who were flying through the air to kill him.

Clint managed to smash one of them across the head and then he was brought down by the weight of the other. A knife flashed in the moonlight and he threw an arm up to block the killing slash. An Apache grunted with pain and their arms locked; the knife gleamed and inched downward as the Indian leaned on it. His face was a hideous mask of hatred and his lips were pulled back to reveal his teeth. Clint watched the blade inching toward his neck. He was not in the best of condition, still weak from the earlier loss of blood, and his strength was just not back in his arms yet.

He did the only thing he could do to save his life and that was to jam a thumb into the Apache warrior's eye.

Even an Apache will scream when he is in agony. This one was no exception. The warrior's head rocked back and Clint was momentarily forgotten. He rolled, threw the Indian aside, and then snatched the first thing he could get his hands on, a rock. He jumped on the man and smashed him once across the forehead. The Apache was incredibly tough. He tried to reach for Clint, but the Gunsmith bashed him again and now the man lay still.

Clint twisted around and scrambled to his feet. He raised the buffalo rifle, shattered stock and all, and he braced himself for whatever was to come next.

It was over. He knew it was. No more owls hooting in the night; no more terrible screams and flying bronze bodies coming out of the semidarkness with only one purpose and that to kill.

Clint dropped the rifle and reloaded his gun. Both mules were dead, pincushioned with Apache arrows.

"Boris." He knelt beside the old prospector, marveling at the ring of bodies surrounding him. Boris had killed at least eight with his hunting knife before they had dragged him to earth.

"Can you hear me?" Two broken arrows protruded from the giant's chest and Clint guessed the huge prospector must have snapped them, just as a man would a pesky fly when he had had important things to do. The arrows alone would have killed a normal man, but deep and vicious knife wounds really did the damage. Boris' face was a mask of blood, for one of them had begun to scalp him while he was yet alive.

"Boris?"

His eyes fluttered open but Clint had watched enough men die to know that Boris could not see him clearly. The prospector gazed upward for a long time before he mumbled, "Can't see the stars anymore, Gunsmith."

"It got cloudy all of a sudden," Clint lied. "The moon went behind the clouds, too. You're going to be all right. We'll get you patched up and—"

"You are the worst liar I ever met in my life," he said,

biting his lip as his body stiffened with a wave of pain. "I'm a dead man. You got to find my daughter, Gunsmith. You got to promise you'll find her and get her away from them."

"Sure."

Boris struggled to pull something bulky from his pocket. The leather pouch finally came out, spilling gold dust and small golden nuggets—a lot of them. Boris chuckled. "And all the time you thought I was half crazy for staying here in hell, didn't you?"

"Yeah, I did," Clint admitted, scooping up as much of the gold dust as he could along with the nuggets and pouring them back into the pouch before he drew the leather thongs tight and gave it to the dying prospector. "That is a lot of gold."

"It's my payment to you for finding my Maria and getting her away from this killing country. See that she is taken care of, will you?"

"I won't take money for it; this gold will go to her."

"Doesn't matter," he said with a sad smile. "Maria knows where this came from and where I keep a pot of gold buried behind the cabin, where no one would ever find it. It's enough gold to take care of a couple of lovebirds like you and Maria the rest of your lives."

Clint smiled. He did not have the heart to tell this man that he had no intentions of marrying anyone, especially a young girl for her gold. "I'll do my best to find and save her, Boris. You got my promise."

"That is good enough for any man." He rolled his head to the side and stared, unseeing. "The mules, they kill both Jug and Sneezer?"

"Got a couple of arrows in them, but they'll be fine."

The giant sighed happily. "Good, I was real worried about that pair. You keep 'em together; they'll never let you down."

"I know. All during the fight they stood there as steady as could be. If they'd tried to run away, I'd be a dead man."

"Mules are better than horses. You ought to ride a mule,

Gunsmith. One might save your life again someday. Get
. . . get away fast. More . . . more'll be comin' soon.''

"I will. How will I know your daughter when I see her?''

"Beautiful and she wears a turquoise ring on her right little
finger. Her . . . her mother's ring. In my other pocket,
you'll see its mate. Wear it. Wouldn't fit over my knuckles
anymore, but I always carry it. Her mother made both.''

The last words he spoke had come in a rush, as if he had
one final gasp of life. When it was gone, he had known there
would be no more. Clint reached into the man's pocket and
found the Indian wedding ring. It was made out of beaten
silver and inscribed with Apache signs he did not understand.
The turquoise itself was dark, a rich blue-green. It fit perfectly on a finger. Now, as Clint laid the man's shaggy head
flat, he swayed.

He climbed up and out of the blood-soaked draw and stared
into the shadowy night. He had granted a dying man's last
wish to rescue his daughter—if, indeed, she wanted to be
rescued.

So now he had one more good reason for hunting down
Taggert. The man was out there somewhere and so were
Maria and Jane Gottman.

My God, he thought, and so are more Apaches and a desert
that stretches as far as the eye can see. Clint squared his
shoulders and walked on. He would get all the water and
leave as soon as he covered Boris with rocks and sand.
Animals would probably dig him up and eat him anyway—if
the Apache didn't discover the corpse first and mutilate it.
But he could do no less than try to give another man a decent
burial; Clint expected that the Apaches would do the same for
their own dead before they began to hunt him down again.

Chapter Nineteen

He had been able to catch only two of the Apaches' ponies, and those only because they were so thin and weak they had no spirit to run.

As dawn broke like a flood of molten metal, Clint rode one pony with only blankets to keep himself from being chafed by the starved animal's backbone. The second pony, a wretched dun with one infected eye, followed close behind carrying every scrap of food Clint could salvage from the Apache camp in addition to what he and Boris had left between them when they were attacked.

Most precious, of course, were the canteens and Apache skin bags holding water, enough water for him and the two ponies for at least two or three days. If Clint had not found a source of new water by then, he knew he would have to shoot the animals and save what water he could be himself.

He tried to think of how far north the desert ran—hundreds of miles, clear to the tough mountains of northern Arizona, which were stark and forbidding. Red Taggert, he was sure, would not go that far. Somewhere up ahead, he would find the man and there would be water, trees, and grass—maybe even a town, an outlaw stronghold. Those kinds of places were not unheard of in the West. Few men spoke of them and those who did rarely lived to talk about them a second time.

"Come on," Clint urged the little pony who moved with its head down close between its legs. "I'll make you a promise, horse—both you and your friend. If you get me to water and carry me and a pair of ladies out of this desert, I will find you both a grassy pasture and pay someone to keep you fat and sassy for the rest of your lives.''

The ponies didn't raise their heads or even blink at his voice. Beaten, driven beyond endurance, they were numb and pitiful little creatures who expected nothing but pain and death at the hands of humans.

Clint found Red Taggert's tracks on the second day—and more important, water on the third. It would be more correct to say that the pony he rode got thirsty and hunted up a tiny desert spring. It was hidden in high rocks by a ridge along the desert floor. Grass covered no more than a twenty-foot circle around the spring before the water vanished back into the sandy earth.

The water was sweet and cool. Clint let the ponies drink their fill and then he drank deeply. Satisfied, he dunked his head into the water and then he took off his shirt and washed himself of the sweat, dirt, and blood. He rinsed his clothes as well and then laid them on a rock to dry. He would climb under a boulder and sleep through the heat of the day and then he would continue on when it cooled a little.

But when he was hanging up his clothes, he spotted something that moved out on the desert floor. It was nothing more than the glint of sunlight on something bright.

Clint dropped to his knees, puting bare flesh on hard rock. He was stark naked. He knew that if he moved he would be seen. The sun beat down unmercifully on his skin and he began to sweat heavily. He remained as still as the rocks.

An agonizing hour passed before he saw another movement, but when he did, he knew that his worst fears were about to come true. It was another Apache, and there were more, many more, and they were coming for him.

Clint took a deep breath and stood up, feeling his flesh already on fire. This time there would be no Boris to stand with. This time there was no giant to swing the great rifle against an attack.

Clint pulled on his dried clothes and he let his ponies drink their fill a second time. He was in no hurry now.

The Apaches were coming. They had found Boris and their dead tribesmen and they had followed his trail with a need for vengeance.

Clint filled all of his water skins and canteens. He was going to give them a chase into these barren hills, and he would make his last stand.

Apaches admired courage. Clint did not know if his measured up to their standards or not. What he did know was that if they were determined to kill him, they would have to pay the price. He counted twenty bullets left for his gun and his goal was to make every last one of them count.

Chapter Twenty

He was down to three bullets and one shot of water. On the rocky slopes that fell away from around him in every direction, he could see at least one Apache, sometimes more.

The contest was almost over. The Apache had tried everything to kill or break him. Nothing had worked, and they had quickly learned that he had night vision equal to their own and his aim was unfailing.

Clint lay trapped in the rock walls of his high fortress and panted like a mountain lion finally brought to bay, knowing its end was near. His ponies had died. Now they were thickly covered with flies and their stench was overpowering.

Three bullets and one shot of water. He had not drunk in quite some time. His eyes were blistered by the glare of sun on white rocks and sand, and his hands were shaking from his thirst and fatigue. Today, he thought, is the day I die. He had been thinking for a long time that he would save his last bullet for himself. He had even taken it out of his gun and placed it in his shirt pocket so that, if an attack came, he would not forget to save it for himself when he was about to be overrun.

There were still at least ten Apaches out there. He could never count them exactly, for they moved constantly. It was nearing sundown and they were coming again. Clint took the third bullet out of his shirt pocket and plugged it into the cylinder of his gun. He reconsidered killing himself in order to avoid the agonies of indescribable torture. Killing himself went against his thinking. Now that the decision was at hand, he decided that he would use the third bullet on the last

Apache and that he would fight so hard that they would have no choice but to kill him in the heat of the battle.

His chin involuntarily slipped to his chest and Clint dozed. It could not have been for long because when he raised his head the sun was just diving into the horizon and the sky was bloodred. Clint started, blinked his eyes, and stared.

The Apaches were gone! They had to be! There was no reason for them to hide from him now, they had given that strategy up.

Clint stood. He was so weak he had to support himself by hanging on to a rock. He stared out at the hills and saw nothing that moved. He stumbled around the entire perimeter of his fortress, giving his enemy an unobstructed shot at him, and still he saw and heard nothing. The Apaches were gone!

Clint wanted to laugh and he wanted to cry. He climbed over the natural rock wall he had fortified, and he bowed his head in thanksgiving. He raised his canteen and saluted the beautiful, dying sunset and tossed down his last swallow of water.

And, then, looming out of the final haze of desert light, a rider appeared—a tall slender figure on a palomino. Several moments later, rising out of the dark hills behind him rode five—no, at least ten more with rifles.

Clint swayed with disbelief at the incredible sight. He ground his cracked and blistered knuckles into his eyes and looked again, hoping that this was a nightmare, a fabrication of a mind finally pushed too far. But it was no dream. And no nightmare. He now had hope. He could hear the squeak of saddle leather, the cough of a horse, the sound of shod hooves, the jingle of silver Mexican spurs. Because of the dying light, he could see none of them distinctly; they were silhouettes on the slopes, but even though he did not know who they were, he knew that without them he would be a dead man.

The Gunsmith leaned back against the rocks for support and waited. His mind and his body were so weakened by the lack of food and water that he did not even try to imagine who these people might be. It occurred to him that they might also want to kill him, but if they did, they, too, would find that he would not die without a fight. He still had those three bullets.

As they drew closer, he pushed away from the rocks and stood as tall and straight as he could because he wanted them to know he had faced death many times and he was not afraid.

Chapter Twenty-One

The rider stopped at twenty yards. He dressed like a vaquero, yet wore a Stetson instead of a sombrero. He sat his horse with the peculiar gracefulness of a natural horseman; he was a slender, prepossessing figure whose face, though shadowed, showed a sharp outline as if cut from granite.

His voice was surprisingly soft, though deep and resonante. "Who," the rider asked, "are you?"

"My name is Clint Adams."

"No," the man said after his eyes covered the field of dead Apaches, "I think your name is the Gunsmith. Is that not true, señor?"

Clint nodded.

The rider pushed back his hat and swung down from his horse. He was surprisingly young, no more than twenty. They were of equal height and weight. When the young man smiled, he was exceedingly good-looking and probably Mexican or Spanish with some English blood.

The rider stuck out his hand and barked in Spanish for his riders to make camp soon, but to do it away from this place, so they would not be plagued by the smell of death.

"My name is Mando Santana," he boasted. "And I am the son of a Spanish grandee and great lady. I am here to save your life, but I must warn you that I regretfully insist on payment, for I have men who do not ride into hell solely for the pleasure of my company and charm."

"As you can see, I have nothing."

"I think you have much." Mando grinned. "Surely there is value to the life of one who is so famous?"

Clint cracked a smile. The way that Mando had expressed himself made it hard to feel threatened, yet it seemed obvious enough from looking at the riders who now had circled them that this was one tough band of fighters. They had to be. No one survived and prospered in Apache country unless he was exceptionally fierce. And the way the Indians had disappeared demonstrated beyond words the measure of their respect for these ten—and a woman, Clint saw with surprise. A very pretty woman.

Mando saw him looking at the woman. "Her name is Señorita Rita Sanchez. Lovely, is she not?"

At the mention of her name, Rita smiled and her eyes caressed Clint's face like a soothing kiss. Despite his condition, Clint felt a stir of interest, for it had been a long, long time since he had seen anyone with such animal magnetism as this woman.

Mando smiled. "She likes you, too; it is easy to see. You look as if you need a woman's care, Gunsmith."

"In the shape I am in, a woman like that would be the death of me."

Mando Santana thought that very funny, but when he finished laughing, he turned serious again. "I am sorry to keep bringing up something like money, but we are here because of it, and I do not try to deceive you. I am a man of honesty and great need. If I wanted to kill you, I would tell you first, then do it."

"If I refused to pay you, would you try?"

Mando looked at his men who had suddenly grown very attentive. "Yes," he said almost regretfully, "I would because you would not be telling me the truth, not meeting honesty with honesty. I know you have gold with you. We found some that spilled by your tracks. I want it all."

"It is for a girl. It was given to me by her father as payment for rescuing her from an outlaw by the name of Red Taggert. Perhaps you have heard of him."

"I have. I do not like him. But he is not what we are talking about, señor. We are talking about the gold that I and my poor friends want for driving away the Apaches today and saving the life of one so famous."

"It is not mine to give," Clint told him with easy firmness. "If the girl wants to give it to you for helping her, that is fine. But I can't."

"For the girl to give it to me, she would have to be here. She is not. You are."

"Then," Clint said, "I ask you to help me to get her away from Taggert. After she is free, I will personally ask her to give you the gold."

"Suppose," Mando said slowly, "I agree to do this, and then she refuses?"

Clint shrugged. "Then you would probably take her gold."

"You are right! But would you try to stop me, after what I have done today?"

"I don't know," Clint said honestly. "I might."

Mando frowned deeply. "If I ask my men about this—they do not speak English like me and Señorita Sanchez—they would tell me to kill you now and take the gold. Much cleaner that way. But I should like to have your famous gun as a gift, a special show of friendship and appreciation."

"No," Clint said softly. "I will not give it to you."

"Hmmm!" Mando Santana scowled. "I think I will not tell my men about this until I have had time to sleep on it tonight. I think better in the morning and am less given to anger. Perhaps you might be more agreeable in the morning too, huh, Gunsmith?"

"I could use food and drink," he admitted.

"Then you shall have both, and I shall leave the beautiful Señorita Sanchez with you tonight!"

"Uh-uh," Clint said wearily. "I could do her no justice because of my physical weakness. Perhaps some other time."

"I think you underestimate yourself," Mando said,

"while perhaps overestimating the ability of my own small force. We are only a third the size—not even that—of Taggert's band. What you offer seems like very little payment for great risk. Is that not true? How much gold do you have?"

"Maybe a pound." There was no sense in hiding the fact.

"That is not enough for what you ask. I am afraid you leave us with very little choice but to . . ."

"Wait!" Clint could not afford to let the man finish that sentence. Once done, there could not be any turning back without loss of pride. "What if there was a chance for more gold? Much more."

"Now that," Mando Santana said, "would make a great difference to all of us, a very great difference. Where is this other gold?"

"That is a secret I shall not tell you until I have the girl safe and another woman by the name of Mrs. Jane Gottman."

"Another man's wife?"

"She is a widow."

Mando frowned. "I offer you the señorita; you tell me you are too weak for her services; now, you tell me you want us to save for you two other woman. I am getting confused, señor!"

"It is a long story," he said patiently. "But I will tell you where this other gold is if you help me."

"I will think about it tonight." Mando yawned. "I have had little rest. I need sleep."

"We both do."

Mando nodded. He threw down a canteen and ordered his men to leave Clint food and blankets.

"I will hear this long story of yours tomorrow morning and then I will decide."

"Good night."

Clint watched them ride into the darkness. The moment they were out of sight, he fell to his knees, uncorked the canteen, and drank deeply. He choked on the fiery tequila and his eyes stung, but he drank more anyway. Then he unwrapped a piece of leather and gobbled down some spicy meat. He spread out the blankets thrown to him and undressed down to his underclothes. His own clothes were stiff with salty sweat and hot, and he was glad to be rid of them. This was the first night in a long, long while that he did expect an Indian attack.

Clint gazed at the heavens and drank a little more tequila, feeling it eat away the pain from his abused body. He sure hoped Mando decided to accept his offer. With food and something to drink, life was almost worth hanging onto again.

He wearily closed his eyes.

"Señor Gunsmith?"

Clint opened his eyes and rolled for his gun.

"No, señor!"

She was standing only ten feet from him. In her arms she held a bottle of something and a bundle of clean clothes.

He lowered his gun, then set it aside and reached for the clothes. She smiled shyly in the moonlight and instead pushed the bottle at him.

Clint took a sip. It was wine and it was a little sweeter than he liked but excellent, so he drank more. Almost instantly, he felt strong and more alert, alert enough to realize that she was undressing herself and coming to kneel beside him.

"No," Clint said gently. "You see, I am in pretty poor shape and I don't think . . ."

He was going to tell her that he doubted he had the strength or the will to service her, but when he followed her eyes down to his underpants, he saw that a large erection mocked his words.

She giggled. Clint chuckled and drank some more of whatever kind of love medicine she had brought him. When the woman's lips touched his own and her tongue darted out, Clint reached for her.

"Señorita," he whispered into her ear, "I think I am about to be physically resurrected."

Chapter Twenty-Two

She was hot-blooded and not the kind of woman who liked a lot of foreplay. What she wanted was good old sex. Rita Sanchez tore her mouth from his, grabbed his shorts, and yanked them off in a rush. Before Clint quite got over that surprise, she grabbed him with both her hands, then climbed on top of him, and began to work his cock back and forth between her legs.

She was on her knees, head thrown back, using him to prime herself, and in a matter of minutes, she was hot and set. She threw her head forward so that her long hair hung around her face and almost to his chest. "You like?" she growled.

"Damn right," he told her, surprised at how her savagery had excited him.

"Me, too, Gunsmith. Now we go faster!"

It wasn't a statement; it was a command. The thought occurred to him that he was being used. He was trying to decide if he liked that feeling when she sat down on him hard and he felt himself drive into her wet slickness until his length was completely buried.

Rita bit her lip and writhed with pleasure. She began to work up and down on him, knees locked against his ribs. The girl framed in the moonlight was a sight Clint knew right then he would never forget.

Rita Sanchez was not the most beautiful woman he had ever entered, nor was her figure classic, but she was hard and firm and strong. And most of all, she loved loving.

She began to grunt as she moved faster. And then she was

115

speaking some kind of singsong thing that was obviously exciting her all the more because she laughed wickedly and there was a smile on her lips whenever she looked down at him.

Clint slipped his hands under his own buttocks and that drove his cock in farther, and Rita squealed with approval, for she had obviously never had any man so large or taken one so deep. The size of him fascinated her. Every ten or fifteen thrusts, she would lift herself completely off him, reach down, grab his wet cock, and speak to it lovingly before she slammed it back into her with fierce possessiveness.

He wanted to make her come first, and he knew that he could. She sweated and rivulets of it ran down her tawny body and dropped on him. Her thighs were slick against his ribs and the sound of their union and their flesh made a slurping sound that Clint liked.

She was moving faster and faster. Her fingers were kneading his chest and her lips were pulled back from her teeth. She was breathing as if she had run for miles and the gibberish she spoke was coming in hard bursts as the tempo of their union grew more frenzied.

"Come on, girl!" he said, unable to keep his mouth from her firm breasts. He pulled her down and began to suck and she could no longer speak but began to grunt again louder and faster until he knew she was close to coming undone.

"Now." Clint panted, wondering if he could outlast her, "I'm taking over things."

He rolled her off, and when she fought and protested violently, he jammed his huge member between her legs. She quieted right down like a baby getting a fresh bottle of milk. He was on her now and he knew that she wanted him to give her everything he had.

Clint could be a gentle man on a gentle woman, but Rita Sanchez was not gentle. She was as hard and violent as the land, and she wanted her man to match her ferocity in the act. He was happy to oblige. His lean hips began to piston in and out and he pinned her mouth and let his lips slide across her neck and down over her breasts. He tasted her and he used her and she loved it.

"Ohh . . . ohhh. Gunsmith!" she cried, throwing her arms and her legs around him and letting her body release itself as she lost control.

Clint figured it was the closest thing he would ever know about how cats joined. The woman under him just went crazy as she began to scream and spasm and flail with her arms and her legs. He hung on with all of his strength, and then his own hips were jerking as he filled her with each shuddering stroke.

He clutched her as much out of self-preservation as passion until her body finally went limp in his arms. She was breathing so hard he thought she might faint, but she did not. In five minutes she gently pushed him off herself, then climbed back on him, grabbed his sagging cock, and crammed it back inside.

"It will be ready again soon? I think I want it again very soon, Gunsmith."

Clint's eyes snapped open and this time he pushed her away. "Uh-uh," he said in earnest. "In my condition, once a night is all that I can stand. That's it, señorita. No more tonight!"

She pouted. "You can make a woman feel very, very good!"

He chuckled and then studied her. "Thank you," he said. "I have always tried to please."

"This Señora Goodman. . ."

"Gottman."

"Sí, she is the one. Is she your woman?"

"No."

"Then Rita Sanchez will be your woman."

"I don't think that would be very smart on my part. What would Mando Santana say to that?"

Rita rolled away laughing. "He is my brother! He doesn't care what we do!"

Clint sat up, wide awake now. "He's your brother?"

Come to think of it, he thought, there is a physical re-
semblance.

"Sí! I ride with him, fight with him. We take much gold
back to save our mother and father. *Comprendes?*"

"Well, I'll be damned," Clint said with amazement. "But
he said that your parents were royal people. No offense, but
which is it?"

"Mando lies a little sometimes. Our mother was a peasant.
Our father is a Spanish grandee who gave our mother some
money for our care. He took Mando away when he was ten
and sent him to good schools, but me, I was just forgotten and
stayed with my mother and worked. I made much money
seeing my father's friends at night. I did fine until mother
died. I hate father. He is now in prison. I love him now
because he has nothing. Now, he is a good man. Before
. . ." She spat into the dust. Her meaning was clear.

"Well, I'll be damned," Clint said again as he stared at her
and thought about the fascinating story.

"Not damned, but dead if you don't tell us where the gold
is buried. After you do," she said, "I make sure you live and
marry me."

"Why would you want to marry me? You don't even know
who I am."

"You are a good man with gun, sí?" She giggled.
"You're a damned good man with this gun, too," she said,
reaching for him.

Clint batted her hand away and pulled on his shorts. "I've
got to get some sleep," he explained. "Tomorrow is going to
be a hard day."

"A short one for you, I think, if you don't tell Mando
where the gold is. Why not tell me now and I'll tell him?"

Clint shook his head. "I'll tell you when I have Jane
Gottman and Maria safe. Then, you can have it all."

The woman laid down beside him and snuggled up close.
"I wake you a little early just in case you want to make love
again. Sí, Gunsmith?"

He started to tell her that he would not appreciate that very much at all, but then he thought that Mando Santana might have him executed in the morning. If that were the case, what the hell was the use of saving his strength?

He reached back and patted her muscular haunches, ''Sí,'' he said.

''Thank you. You won't be sorry.''

He smiled in the darkness. That he wouldn't be sorry and the sun rising in the morning were the only two things he knew for dead certain were absolutely true.

Chapter Twenty-Three

Mando Santana studied them with a smile of brotherly amusement. "I see that you were not too weary to enjoy Señorita Sanchez."

Clint stood up and looked him right square in the eye. "Señorita Santana, don't you mean? Yes, your sister is a fine woman."

Mando Santana stiffened as if he had been slapped. His eyes shifted quickly to those of Rita, whose angry glare matched his own, and she said defiantly, "If this man is to die, what does it matter that he knows? If he is alive, I want to marry him."

Mando scowled and waved his hand with distraction. "Let us see if he shall live before we talk of such things."

Clint took a deep breath. "I cannot tell you where the gold is because only Maria knows. To find the gold, we must rescue her. There is no other way. Afterward, it will be up to her to decide if she will share it."

"Sounds like a bad deal to me," Mando grumbled. "Maybe I should take the pouch of gold that you carry and forget the rest of this business."

He looked at his sister. "Rita, did you steal the gold like I told you?"

She shook her head stubbornly. "If I had done it, he would never marry me."

"He will never marry a *puta* like you anyway!"

Rita walked up and spat at him, and when Mando's hand drew back to slap her face, Clint caught his wrist in a grip of

121

iron. ''She is your sister; treat her with respect.''

His warning was flat and deadly and it caught Mando Santana by surprise. ''You want to die for sure?'' he asked with one eyebrow cocked.

''We all die sooner or later,'' the Gunsmith said, releasing the man's wrist and stepping back with his hand poised near his gun.

Mando glanced at his men, who were watching them from a short distance. ''Gunsmith, you have made a big mistake. If I do not try to kill you, my men will think I am afraid, and they will not follow me. I have no choice but to try to kill you now.''

Clint saw the way of it. It was a deep sense of macho and honor that was going to cause one of them to die in the next moment. He knew that he could outdraw this handsome young man, but that would surely spell his own death as the others opened fire to avenge the death of their leader.

Clint suddenly pretended great fear. He took a shaky step back and then threw his hands up into the air. He was the picture of a coward.

Mando blinked with surprise. Then, as he followed Clint's gaze toward his men, he smiled. ''Ah, I see. You do this for them!''

''That's right. Play along and we can both get out of this.''

''But you will have lost face,'' Rita protested.

''I'll make it up when we overtake the Taggert gang,'' Clint told her. ''Until then, they can think whatever they want of me. I don't give a damn.''

''I do not understand that,'' Mando said frankly, ''but it does solve the problem, sí?''

''Sí. Now, have we got a deal?''

Mando nodded. ''But my men will think you are a coward. I cannot let my sister sleep with you again until you have shown them otherwise. To do so would bring us shame.''

Clint shrugged. ''We have a long and a hard ride across this desert. I need my strength for that. I am sorry, señorita.''

"So am I," she said, "but I can sneak to you late at night for I move like a cat."

"I'm sure," he said, "but you make love entirely like another animal, one a lot more vocal."

"Vocal, what does that mean?"

Mando interrupted. "He means you yell and grunt very loudly when he does it to you."

"Oh." She actually looked a little embarrassed. "That, I cannot stop."

"Shall we ride?" Clint asked.

Mando nodded. "I know where they are going—four days ride to the north."

"Have you ever been there before?"

"No, but I have heard of the place. It will be very difficult to attack. I must tell my men there is a great treasure of gold that waits, a treasure worth risking their lives for."

"Then tell them," Clint said, "and let us ride."

The next five days were a nightmare. Clint rode a starved pony. The poor animal should have been carried by him. It was weak and kept stumbling so that Clint could not relax for even a moment lest the beast pitch forward and injure them both. The afternoon heat was almost unbearable, and it did not cool off more than fifteen degrees during the night. They pushed hard, stopping only for a few hours in the middle of the afternoon and then making up that time in the morning and evening hours.

Rita Santana was able to reach his blankets twice without being seen by a guard. On both occasions, there was little time, but what time there was she used to the fullest. The woman was insatiable and hotter than the Arizona sun when Clint entered her. He often looked at her when they rode during the day, and despite his fatigue he always had a stiff erection. He didn't think any man was up to a steady diet of Rita, but one could die happily trying.

When they awoke on the morning of the fifth day, Mando

told them they would travel the last few miles to the outlaw stronghold on foot. He also told everyone to bring ammunition and knives because they would fight before they returned.

Clint only had three bullets for his gun, but he figured that if he could reach Taggert or get close enought to his men, some would have the same caliber ammunition. Then he would be ready to go to war. Mando had given him an old musket loaded with lead pellets, and though primitive, it could blow the hell out of a man at close range.

He started to move beside Rita as they filed out of camp, but one of Mando's band pushed him roughly aside. Clint almost lost his self-control. Five days of eating contempt and keeping a lid on his temper had worn him down, as had the unrelenting heat; he was ready to fight.

But Rita checked him with her hand and he read the concern in her eyes. They were about to go against a much larger force and they needed every gun that they could muster if they were to be victorious.

Clint nodded at her and fell back to the rear of the line of men, the lowliest of the bunch. He chided himself for not having taken a stronger grip on himself. Up ahead in the mountains where a few pine trees actually seemed to exist, there awaited Jane Gottman and, he hoped, Maria. Clint absently polished the turquoise ring on his finger. The girl would recognize it and know that he was sent by her father.

Their lives are in my hands, he thought, and here I almost risked my chances over a matter of pride, of who walks before whom.

Clint wiped his forehead and kept walking. If he ever got out of this hell, he would never come back to the desert.

Never!

Chapter Twenty-Four

They stopped for a short rest, and after a few minutes, Mando Santana sauntered to Clint, who stood apart from the others. The man rolled a cigarette and smiled. "It is a little cooler. We are climbing to a plateau, Gunsmith. The temperature will not reach much over a hundred today."

Clint nodded. It was cooler, though it would still get hot enough to fry eggs on the rocks. He shaded his eyes and stared ahead toward the ring of dark and forbidding mountains that loomed just up ahead.

"Don't you think," Clint said, "that it is time to tell me what kind of place these outlaws are holed up in?"

"You will see soon enough. These mountains right before us, they form a volcano that has been dead for centuries." Mando stopped, reached down, and picked up a piece of volcanic rock. "Long ago, I think, this was very hot."

Clint nodded. The volcanic rock was heavy, yet riddled with air holes.

Mando pitched the rock aside. "This place where the outlaws live is very beautiful. I have seen it but have never been down inside. No one goes inside except for those Red Taggert calls friend, and I have never been his friend. In fact, you might say that we are after the same business."

"Are you? Taggert robs banks and preys on helpless women. Do you?"

"We take gold or silver from whoever has it. We only kill when someone resists. I make no excuses. I must do this to save my father's life."

"How much money do you need to ransom him from the prison?"

"Ten thousand dollars."

Clint whistled softly. "Your father must have been a very dangerous man."

"In some ways he is. You can buy many guns and outfit many soldiers for that much money, Gunsmith."

"Is your father a revolutionary?" Clint knew that Mexico was a hotbed of revolution and had been for many years. The peons were starving on lands unfit to farm, and the rich, ruling class lived in lavish, protected communities.

"My father is an intellectual, a scholar. His weapons are his words, his letters. There are many who say he is quite harmless as long as he is made to keep his silence."

"Then why do they keep him a prisoner?"

"Because he has something inside of him that will not be stilled. I call it the conscience of a people. There are always a few who speak for the many."

"And you, Mando, are you also outspoken?"

The handsome young man smiled. He drew his gun and shook it with pride. "I am a fighter. I have no patience for words alone—not when guns and bullets get things done much faster. But guns and soldiers cost a lot of money."

"Maybe Red Taggert has a great deal of gold. It will be enough to buy your father's freedom, and then you can let Maria keep what her father prospected for her."

Mando thought that over carefully. "It is possible. I am not greedy. We will see, Gunsmith. Right now, I am only concerned for the lives of my sister and my soldiers."

"Why do you allow your sister to come along on this? It is too dangerous for a woman."

Mando laughed. "You have seen her mount you in the middle of the night and you could not believe her savagery. Is this not true?"

Clint blushed a little. "I would not call it savagery, but she is like no woman I have ever had before."

"Or will have again. Let me tell you this," he whispered. "Maria is the same in a battle as she is on a blanket. I would not trade her for three others. And besides, if I told her not to come, she would laugh or spit in my face. I can tell her nothing. Rita does what she wants, how she wants, when she wants. She would kill any man who tried to rule her, even you."

"How do I tell her that I do not want to marry her, providing, that is, we are victorious?"

"I do not know. That is your problem."

"Thanks," Clint said dryly before he walked away.

Late that afternoon, they reached the mountains, and now Mando called a meeting in the shadows of the volcano. He spoke to his men in Spanish. They listened attentively while he gestured and talked to them with more than a little passion in his voice.

Clint could not catch the exact meaning, for his Spanish was very limited, but he could pick up enough and tell by the gestures that Mando Santana was warning his soldiers that the outlaw stronghold would be guarded and that they must seek out the sentries tonight. Mando drew his own knife and made a slashing motion across his throat with one hand, while the other cupped his mouth. The picture was stark and the meaning very clear. The soldiers must find the guards tonight and kill them without allowing the alarm to be sounded.

In the morning, at dawn, they would signal each other from the rim of the volcano and go in fast and silently. They would kill with knives until the first shot rang out, and then they would open fire. With luck, they would have the odds pared down so that they would have an equal chance.

Mando smiled and shook the hands of men who nodded and then silently vanished into the lengthening shadows.

"Rita, you and I will stay together and clear the west rim of sentries. In the morning, we will be down in the volcano and signal the others to join us.''

''And what if a shot is fired in warning tonight?'' Clint asked.

''Then I have told my men to return to their horses if they can reach them before daylight and join up with us later.''

''I am not leaving without Jane Gottman or Red Taggert,'' Clint said stubbornly.

Mando shrugged. ''I am a fighter like you. Neither of us is a fool, Gunsmith. A true warrior knows when he must run so that he can return and taste victory another day. A fool dies for nothing.''

''I'll try to remember that,'' Clint said with an ill-concealed smile of amusement. He thought of the many gunfights and the men he had been forced to kill over the years. It was not that Mando was wrong, only that the man was barely out of his boyhood and still had a great deal to learn.

They started up the steep volcano, heading toward the rim. The slope was choked with volcanic rock and ash and it must have had some richness to it because there were scrubby trees on the lower elevations and towering pines up toward the rim. Clint stared at the pines. He had begun to think he might never see another green tree. They looked magnificent.

And he could smell something good besides the pine fragrance and he wondered if it were grass and water.

He gazed back on the sweep of the blistered desert. I am not leaving here on the run, he vowed. I would rather face any man than face that desert without water.

Chapter Twenty-Five

The guard was silhouetted against the lip of the rim.

He was stupid to expose himself that way, but the sunset was spectacular and he was enjoying the show. Clint watched Mando and Rita move up on him through the rocks like a pair of panthers. He saw the guard turn momentarily at the sound of a rolling pebble and then stiffen.

Clint drew in his breath, and just as the man was about to reach for his gun, Rita stood up. She was naked to her waist and hugging her breasts, cowering like a frightened child.

The man gaped. The sunset was forgotten and he grinned and came quickly down the slope to her. He grabbed her arm and pulled it away to expose a breast, and when he covered it with his greedy mouth, Rita slipped the knife out of her skirt and drove it up into his chest.

The outlaw died, pulling Rita down with him. She stabbed him once again. Then she cleaned the blade on his pants, stood up, and walked over to reclaim her blouse.

Rita would not meet Clint's eyes when he looked at her, and he did not know what to say. The killing had been violent, calculated, and shocking even to the Gunsmith. It had seemed so inevitable, too, as if Rita Santana had done it all before.

"This," Mando said when they crawled to the edge of the volcano's rim, "is what we seek."

Clint stared down at the sight, hardly believing his eyes. It was a great circular valley, one perhaps two miles

129

across, and he saw it contained a big pond of water and was filled with grass, cattle, and horses.

"Duke!" he whispered happily. "That's my horse."

"The fine black one?"

"Yes!" Clint grinned. "He looks fat and sleek. He looks a lot better than I do."

Mando nodded. "Even so, he will be glad to see you again, Gunsmith."

Clint agreed. He and the black gelding had been through a hell of a lot of bad times, but this might just have been the worst and it was not even over yet.

Clint turned his attention back to the valley itself. He saw houses, a blacksmith shop with a forge and bellows, and several lean-tos and sheds, perhaps a dozen, all small and constructed mostly of rock walls and timber roofs. There were corrals and a thatch-covered porch that shaded crude furniture, a bar, and some tables where ten or twelve outlaws were drinking. When the wind shifted, he could hear the music of a fiddle and banjo and one or two couples were dancing on hard-packed dirt.

"Amazing," Clint said, "absolutely amazing. I have seen a few such places in my day, but nothing to match this one."

"It used to belong to the Apache, but they were slaughtered five years ago. For a long time, they tried to take it back, but they never succeeded. As you can see, the houses and sheds are beyond rifle range. Taggert and his men can drink at the bar and not be in danger. They have water and cattle to eat. The slopes are too steep for horsemen to ride down during a mounted attack."

"Where do riders enter?"

Mando pointed out a cut in the lip that was hardly visible because it was blocked. "The outlaws have four giant oxen that they yoke together to drag a huge boulder in and out of that cut. It is the only place that a man can enter on horseback."

"So," Clint said, "it is the perfect natural fortress."

"I think it is as perfect as God would allow," Mando said. "How many men do you see?"

"I count sixteen. We can bet there are almost that many more inside the houses."

"Seventeen," Rita said. "You missed the man and the woman making love under the tree beside the pond."

Clint smiled with embarrassment when his eyes touched upon the pair wildly coupling on the grass. "Excuse me," he said, "but you are right. I wonder how many are inside and where is Red Taggert right now?"

Again Rita spoke. Study the couple by the pond more closely. Can you not see his red hair?"

It was Red all right and the woman underneath him was Mrs. Gottman.

Rita laughed, and it had a hard, cutting sound. "If you were in love with her, I am sorry for you, but she does not look to me to be a woman who wants to be rescued from her outlaw."

"No," Clint said with a frown, "at the moment, I'd have to say that being rescued is the farthest thing from her mind."

He looked at Rita Santana. "I never loved the widow. I just felt responsible for her getting taken off that stage. She was to be a witness against Taggert."

"I do not think," Rita said impishly, "that she would be a very good one anymore."

Clint had to grin at the irony of all this. He had been deeply concerned about Mrs. Gottman and how she must have been suffering at the mercy of the outlaw. Now, to find her like that, so obviously enjoying herself . . . well, it just changed things considerably.

"Come on," Mando said with a knowing smile. "We need to clear this part of the rim of guards before it is completely dark . . . unless you cannot bear to miss the show they are putting on."

Clint scowled and the brother and sister laughed softly as they melted into their surroundings. As he turned, Clint took one last glance at the couple because now Mrs. Gottman was on top and it was for sure she was enjoying herself.

Some witness!

Chapter Twenty-Six

The Santanas eliminated two more guards along the west edge of the rim and one guard provided Clint's replacement ammunition. It was the break that the Gunsmith needed. Three bullets were not going to do a whole lot of good down there. The outlaws were gunmen themselves; they would not be taken or killed easily.

Darkness blanketed the land, but the stars, as they had every night he had been in the desert, flooded the sky like tiny beads of mercury.

Clint moved off to lie by himself. Mando had told him that they would be moving down into the valley several hours before dawn. He wondered if they would be successful and what he was going to do with Jane Gottman. Never mind her, he told himself. Concentrate on Red Taggert. Remember what he did to Hank Tilson and that stagecoach driver. And what about Boris' daughter? Would she be down there, too? And if she were not, what then?

Clint took a deep breath. With Jane Gottman, Maria, and Rita, he had more women to worry about than he could rightly stand. And on top of everything, he wondered what Mando's soldiers might do if there were no gold to be plundered after a victory against great odds.

He looked forward to tomorrow. One way or another, it was going to tie up a lot of loose ends that were cluttering his thoughts.

"Señor Gunsmith?"

He turned his head to see Rita close beside and reaching for him. Clint stifled a groan. He needed rest tonight, not more loving.

"Hold me, please," she whispered softly.

Clint blinked. This was not the demanding, wild woman who had come to his side in the nights before now. "Is something wrong?"

She looked up at him and he could see that her eyes were shiny with tears. "You are crying," he whispered.

She nodded. "You did not think I could be hurt, that I could cry like other women. But I can."

"Why?"

"Because of what I saw on your face after I killed that first guard. It was . . . Seeing your face then was like taking the blade into my own heart. You would not even look at me! I know this to be true."

Clint held her tighter and kissed her tears away. He had been shocked, though he did not realize it had been so apparent. "Rita, I am sorry. You did what you had to do. I know that."

"Then why—"

He kissed her because he was ashamed of himself for hurting her. Without realizing it, he had come to think of her as a killer, as a predator, an animal without emotions, only hungers and passion. He had been wrong.

Clint stroked her long black hair and held her close as he watched the heavens change through the night. He did not try to make love to her this time, for he sensed that no man had ever held Rita Santana tenderly in the darkness. She needed that tonight.

Later when it was time to move, he awakened her and she clung to him for a moment. And then she climbed to her feet and said, "I love you as I have no man in my life."

Clint swallowed hard. He did not know what to say to Rita, so he kissed her once more. Then they followed Mando over the rim of the volcano and down into the outlaw valley.

When the first shafts of light appeared, the three of them

stood out in the open flat of the land and studied the surrounding rim overhead. Slowly Mando's soldiers emerged to raise their rifles in signal. A full circle was made and Clint knew that the walls were cleared of all opposition.

What men they faced were ahead in the houses and maybe asleep under the thatched roof where they drank and danced.

The time was now! Already, Mando's soliders were coming quickly down into the crater of the dead volcano. They must strike within the next ten or fifteen minutes before someone awoke to sound the alarm.

They were still greatly outnumbered and surprise was the edge that would carry them to victory.

Clint waited until all the soldiers had reached the valley floor. He reached out and touched Rita's hand and then the trio parted, each a hunter alone and determined to kill as many as quickly as possible.

The rock houses were dark and silent. He could smell smoke, and somewhere a horse huffed softly. Duke? Clint did not know. Perhaps the great horse sensed his presence and was calling.

The call would have to go unanswered this time. It was a time for dying.

Chapter Twenty-Seven

Clint could see a soldier moving into the nearest house. He heard a choking sound, and then suddenly, when he was still thirty feet away from the house, there was a single shot.

"Charge!" Mando yelled, sprinting forward.

The gunshot had ruined the element of surprise. It was almost daylight now, and Clint could see figures of men, though he could not identify individuals. From the doors and the windows of the houses, outlaws began to fire and those of Mando's soldiers still far out in the grassy meadow knew that they were in desperate trouble. Some found low spots or logs; others nearer to the settlement were able to throw themselves behind sheds and return gunfire. Every one of them understood that they had to finish this thing quickly or they would all be wiped out, for time would work to the advantage of the outlaws whose supply of food and ammunition was greater.

Clint saw a tall, powerful figure running behind the houses toward a barn and yelling for men to rally and fight.

"Taggert!"

The man swung around and his gun stabbed spears of flame in the murky morning light. Clint felt a bullet pluck at his shirt and then he dropped and fired twice. Taggert momentarily staggered and then disappeared behind the hay barn.

Two outlaws jumped out from the doorway of a house and sprinted toward the barn to join their outlaw leader. Clint dropped one of them in midstride. The other turned and tried to empty his gun but couldn't because Clint's bullets were nailing a pattern across his chest and driving him back.

A bullet kicked dirt in Clint's face and he snapped a shot off that spun an outlaw around full circle and sent the man crawling for cover. Clint's gun fell on an empty cylinder and he cussed and quickly reloaded. Everywhere he looked he saw men fighting for their lives. A soldier hurled himself through a window and screamed in a shower of flying glass. Clint heard the screams die suddenly as an outlaw staggered into the doorway, gripped it, and then pitched forward, dead, with a knife protruding from between his shoulders.

A second later, the soldier appeared. His face and arms were sheeted with blood. He wiped his hands clean on his pants and then tried to assault the next house. He didn't make it. Halfway there, he was greeted by the roar of a double-barrel blast that tore him to pieces.

Rita flew across the yard and Clint saw her drop a man with a single shot. Then she pivoted, changed direction with bullets screaming all around her, and flattened herself against a house. A rifle boomed and Rita grabbed her face as rock shards tore into her cheek. She tried to raise her smoking pistol, but there was blood in her eyes. That's when Clint jumped up and his gun began to explode with anger and death. The man with the rifle never had a chance. His second shot went straight up into the air as Clint's bullet caught him in the sternum and hurled him back through an open doorway. Clint scooped up Rita and carried her behind a water trough.

Bullets began to probe for them. Clint kept his head down and listened to the lead slamming into the wood. Again, a rifle boomed and this time the slug came right on through both sides of the trough and struck Rita in the side.

"Damn you!" Clint raged, rising up and firing until his gun was empty and the rifle was silent.

"Rita!"

"Get out of here," she begged, "before someone with a rifle kills you!"

"Not without you," he vowed, reloading and then daring to scoop up a double handful of water to wash the blood away from her face. "It's only about thirty feet to the nearest shed and I am taking you with me."

"No, please!"

Another rifle slug splintered its deadly way through the trough. To remain here another moment was to die. He picked up the protesting girl and began to run.

It seemed like a thousand miles to the cover of the shed. Clint heard and felt the swarm of bullets that immediately sought him out as he raced forward. His lungs and legs strained, he thought he was going to make it until one of his legs suddenly stopped working properly, and he was going down—still a good ten feet short of cover.

But Rita was spilling forward out of his arms and rolling toward cover. She would live and . . . He looked up and she was coming for him!

"Get back!" he shouted, trying to swing around and return some gunfire.

He felt her hands on his arm, felt his body being pulled forward, and he heard her grunts as she gave herself to save him. Clint holstered his gun and tried to cover the final distance. One of the outlaws appeared and his gun lifted for what seemed to be a killing shot. Clint saw the man and shouted a warning for Rita to drop him and run.

She could not. It was too late, and when the outlaw opened fire, her own pistol was still in its holster. She shielded Clint and took the bullets.

He felt each one of them strike her, felt the breath and the life being ripped from her young, passionate body. Clint cursed, and when the hammer on the outlaw's gun clicked against an empty cylinder, Clint pulled out his own pistol, dragged it across the dirt, and shot the grinning sonofabitch right in the mouth. One minute he had teeth; the next minute there was just an empty, bloody hole in his face, and he was going over backward.

Clint encircled Rita with one arm and crawled, dragging her the rest of the way to safety.

He held her and the pain in his heart was greater by far than that in his leg. She died without speaking; her eyes remained open to tell of her love and devotion to the Gunsmith.

"I love you, too," he whispered, reloading his gun once more. "And they shall all pay for this, for you and for Hank Tilson and for me!"

Clint holstered his gun for the moment it took to bandage his leg. There was a neat hole through the calf muscle. It would pain him for a long while, but unless it became infected, it would be all right.

The Gunsmith leaned over and kissed Rita good-bye; then, slowly, he pushed himself up against the shed and palmed his gun. He was grim and gaunt and never more deadly. He did not know if Mando was still alive or who was winning this raging battle. All he knew was that he had a score to settle with Red Taggert and now he knew where to find him.

It was a score that was long overdue.

Chapter Twenty-Eight

Clint tested his leg and found that it would hold him up, though he would not be able to run or throw himself sideways very quickly. The way bullets were flying, that was going to be a rather serious liability, but there was nothing he could do about it.

His gun was loaded and he was ready. Instead of waiting for a momentary lull in the battle the way an inexperienced fighter might, he waited until the battle was hottest and everyone was fighting for his life. That's when he pulled his hat down low and hobbled toward the shed nearest the barn.

It was a gamble that he won. Clint plastered himself against the shed. He could hear voices just around the corner. He raised his weapon and then spun around the corner to see two outlaws blasting away. It was not Clint's style to shoot men in the back, so he hollered, "Drop 'em!"

The outlaws swung around to fire, but they barely got their weapons up when Clint's gun was bucking in his fist. The pair fell. When they struck the dirt floor, they did not move.

Clint studied the barn, wondering exactly how many outlaws were in it with Red Taggert. They had set up a barricade across the front door, pushed some wagons over on their sides, and looked as if they could withstand any kind of frontal attack.

But there had to be a back door or a loft or some other way to get in, and maybe he could surprise them from behind. Clint moved to the rear of the shed and kicked out the back

141

wall. He had pushed his luck far enough by trying to advance across the open yard. He squeezed through the wall and then headed along a line of structures right up to the back of the barn.

There was a huge set of double doors. When Clint threw them open, all he faced was a wall of hay. It would be impossible to burrow through the stuff in time to be of any use. Just as bad, there was no loft opening he could climb through. The barn was packed solid with hay; the walls bulged with the stuff that would keep the outlaw herds and horses in good shape through the winter months when the grass wilted.

A man suddenly charged around the corner of the barn and almost collided with him. Surprised, they both drew. Clint's gun came up an easy winner.

"Mando!" Clint blurted.

The young man flashed him a smile, and his gun slipped back into his holster. "Now, I know why you are the Gunsmith," he said with reverence. "I am fast, but I would not clear leather against you."

"Never mind that. Any ideas how we get to them without facing that barricade?"

Mando must have had the same idea about coming in the rear door and sneaking up on Taggert and his men from behind. "No," he said bleakly. "If we had dynamite, I would throw it over the barricade."

"Well," Clint said tightly, "we don't have dynamite, but I know that you have some matches and cigars. How about a smoke, Mando?"

The young man grinned. Coolly, he rolled two and gave one to Clint who puffed the tip to glowing before he walked about five feet down the side of the barn and shoved the cigarette through a crack in the wall to fire the hay.

"Why don't you take a walk down the other side of this barn and do a little smoking?"

"See you out front, hombre!"

"As dry as this is, I think it ought to go up like an

oil-soaked torch. I'll give it five minutes, Mando. We can come in from the front corners. Should be interesting.''

Mando nodded. "I won't forget the honor of fighting with you." Clint had to smile at that.

By the time he reached the front of the barn, he had its entire length blazing, and it wouldn't take but a few more minutes for Taggert and his boys to know that they were going to have to leave.

Clint could hear them shouting from around the corner. It sounded as if there were four or five. He looked into the yard and saw that the battle was nearly over. The gunfire had grown sporadic; there were just little pockets of surviving outlaws. So the battle was almost won—would be won if he and Mando could finish off Taggert and these few men.

Clint could see the still form of Rita. His face twisted with fury and he gripped his gun tighter. He wasn't sure if Mando had fired his side of this barn or not, and he wasn't going to wait any longer to find out.

He edged around the corner of the barn. There were five of them, including Red Taggert. They were crouched behind the barricade and getting ready to make a run for it. The smoke was boiling out the front doors. Clint yelled, ''Taggert!''

They swiveled on him like a unit of soldiers, and that's when Clint's gun began to buck in his hand. Taggert was the first to drop. He took two bullets before he went down—given an instant's more time. Clint would have tried hard just to wound the man because he needed answers to questions about Boris' daughter, but there was no extra time, so he merely shot accurately.

The next few minutes were smoke-filled and deadly as he stood his ground and tried to make every bullet count. But he ran one short. When his gun was empty and it seemed certain that he was going to be killed, Mando finally charged around the corner of the barn and saved his life by killing the last outlaw.

For a moment they stood facing each other across the width

of the barn, and Santana did a funny thing; he bowed just slightly before he strode into the billowing smoke, grabbed Red Taggert by the arm, and dragged him out into the yard.

Clint knelt down beside the outlaw and stared at his face. Up close, Taggert was strikingly handsome, with a long, red mustache and bright blue, intelligent eyes that were now red with pain and the effects of the heavy smoke.

"Goes to show you," Red whispered, "a man makes one little mistake, he ends up dying. My mistake was in not going back to make sure you were finished after my boys shot you off the stage."

"Mine was in not killing you the first time we met. Would have saved the lives of some damned fine people."

"We all make . . ." Red grimaced as a spasm shook his body. "We all make mistakes. Better this for me than the gallows."

"Where is Jane Gottman?"

"I'm here," Jane Gottman cried, rushing forward to fall beside the dying outlaw and raise his head to her lap. "Oh, Red, I'm sorry!"

For the first time, his smile faded as he turned his attention from Clint to the woman. "So am I, Jane. You know, I chose you and it wasn't just because of your husband's money. You gotta believe me, baby."

"I believe you," she whispered tearfully.

"Don't let some other hand-handsome sonofabitch take the money away, Jane. Hang on to it."

"I will."

Clint turned away. He did not understand how an intelligent, beautiful woman like her could love a killer like Red Taggert, but then he never confused himself by thinking he understood women—enjoying them was enough.

Clint wished he could walk away and leave the pair alone in their last few minutes together, but he could not. "Taggert, there was a girl, half white and half Apache. She wore a ring like this."

He showed him the turquoise ring the old prospector had

given to him before dying. "She also loved you and her name was Maria. Where is she now?"

Jane Gottman looked up and her face reflected shock and horror. "That girl loved Red, too!"

"That's right," Clint said harshly. "And you can bet that Red didn't fight her off. Maria's father died trying to save her. I promised to find her and see she is taken care of."

Jane stared at Red. The tenderness and tears were replaced by loathing, and she dropped the outlaw's head in the dirt and recoiled. "You—you told me she was in love with one of your men and then you—you sold her, damny you!"

Red feebly tried to raise his trembling hand to touch her once more. "Baby, I—I wanted to tell you the truth, but . . . Jane, she was just a damn little slut who—"

Jane made an animal sound deep in her throat and then, before anyone knew what she was doing, the woman snatched Mando's gun from its holster and shot Red between those lying, bright blue eyes.

Clint was the first to react. He took the gun away from her. "Damn it, Jane! Maybe he could have told me how to find the girl!"

"And her gold," Mando said angrily as he received his gun back. "I need to know where the gold her father buried is!"

They all stared at Jane Gottman who could not tear her hate-filled eyes from the ruined face of Red Taggert.

Clint was reminded once again about the wrath of woman scorned. Red had about been ready to cash it in anyway, but she sure hurried him along.

"I can find her," Jane said. "I can show you where he has taken Maria."

"Who is he?"

"Shatto."

Mando groaned. "That's the end of her. Shatto is an Apache renegade. We don't want to find him."

"I do," Clint said quietly. "I have to. I gave my word on it. How do I find this man, Jane?"

Her chin lifted. "Up to now, I have done everything wrong with my life. Up to now, there is not one single thing that I can say I am proud of. But now, now I am going to help you find this Shatto and I will use my own money, all of it if necessary, to save that poor, lovely girl."

Clint groaned. "I don't suppose there is any use in telling you I wish you would go back to Desert Springs and wait?"

"I'm coming."

The way she said it left no room for argument.

Chapter Twenty-Nine

They buried Rita Santana in the grassy meadow by herself, and Mando was filled with an inconsolable grief.

"I was always the favored one, the one who was well read and educated like my father," he said quietly. "But she was the one of great strength, Gunsmith. She was my sister. I never stopped looking up to her, even when I became a man. Her courage . . . if made mine seem as nothing. She was honest and brave; I both loved and hated her for all those things because I could never match them."

Clint stared at the mound of freshly turned earth and the beautifully carved wooden cross with her name and the span of her life etched lovingly into the wood. He said, "What I liked about her most was that she was honest. There was no guile in the woman. You knew if she hated you or loved you and you knew that she did nothing halfway."

"Would you ever have married her?" Mando asked softly. "She wanted that very much."

He smiled. "I might have. Just might have at that. Rita had a way of turning a man's head and his heart."

"And his body, too. Almost inside out, I think."

Clint said nothing, for it did not seem right to mention that Rita had been one of the wildest, most passionate, and finest women of all times. He thought that he would never have another like her.

He studied Mando. "What did your men say?"

"They found much outlaw gold and dollars here. We split

it evenly. It is enough for them to return to Mexico and live comfortably the rest of their lives."

"Is it enough for you to ransom your father?"

"No, of course not. I need the prospector's buried treasure and that pouch of gold you are carrying for his daughter. What is her name again?"

"Maria."

"Yes, Maria who wears a ring like the one you are wearing, only smaller. Maria, the one who is with Shatto."

"I will not rest until I have found and freed her."

Mando shrugged. "Maybe she likes Shatto. She liked the outlaw, Taggert. What then, Gunsmith?"

"Then I will let her stay with the man."

"And my gold?"

"I will tell her of your father and what you have done. I will ask her to tell us where the gold is buried and we will come back for it. Agreed?"

Mando slipped his hands behind his gunbelt and studied the rim of the volcano. "You know, I almost think I will come back to this place. Maybe . . . maybe I will bring a few good people and we will settle here. There is grass and water; the buildings are all still standing except for the barn that we burned to the ground. Yes, I think I would like that. And my father, he might like it, too."

"The Apache will come again. This is their land and they will never stop trying to take back this place. You had better bring more than just farmers, Mando, if you intend to hold this for your own."

"You are right," he said thoughtfully. "Maybe I will talk to my soldiers and see if they want to buy pieces of land here for their families."

"Buy land?"

"Sí. Right now, I will tell them that in exchange for equal shares of the gold, I want this valley. Later, I will tell them how their families could live in happiness here and that I will sell them plots of land. Since there is only so much of it to sell, I will have to take back most of their shares of the gold in payment!''

''You are a thief,'' Clint grumbled, ''a budding land baron.''

''I know. Maybe my father will make me give them their money back later. But it will feel good to be rich for a little while, eh, Gunsmith?''

Clint laughed. ''I wouldn't know.''

''You have never been rich?''

''I could have been once. I owned half of a rich gold mine in Virginia City, Nevada. I gave it all back to a couple beautiful woman friends.''

''They must have been very, very beautiful for you to give away so much money!''

Clint smiled knowingly. ''Not only beautiful, but very grateful.''

Mando Santana laughed a little obscenely. ''I like that! A man who would give away a fortune for the love of two women at the same time. You will have to tell me all about them someday.''

''Maybe on Shatto's trail, eh, amigo?''

''You are a devil! You remind me that this is a time to pray for the soul of my sister.'' Mando knelt beside the grave. He made the sign of the cross and bowed his head. His soldiers gathered around to do the same.

Clint said a few words of his own for Rita, then he walked away, and left the others to do a better job.

''Look at them,'' Jane said with a hint of disgust in her voice. ''They kill easily. Then they pray as if they will never kill again, all the while wearing their guns, barely able to wait to shoot someone else.''

Clint studied her. He now knew that Jane Gottman had loved Red Taggert and he could not quite forgive her for that. Yet, who was he to judge? Had he not fallen in love with many beautiful women, a few who had themselves killed the same as he? I am in no position to judge anyone, Clint told himself, least of all this woman.

She seemed to read his thoughts. "I guess you must think me pretty contemptible," she said. "I mean, the way I deceived you and the sheriff. But I didn't know that anyone would be killed."

"And what about your husband? Was he supposed to die so that you could inherit his money and then you and Red could go and live happily ever after?"

She slapped him hard across the cheek. Her face was red with fury and her voice shook. "How dare you say that! You didn't know my husband and you do not know me. My husband was a spirit killer, one who foreclosed the mortgages on small, poor people and one who closed businesses by the dozens in Desert Springs. He destroyed lives and ruined marriages. I know he used the wives of several of his friends, let them think they were winning his favor with their bodies, but all the while using them for his pleasure while leaving me to rot unloved. He gloated over his slimy conquests. Red Taggert did the town—hell, he did mankind a favor when he killed Simon."

"All right, so your husband was a slug," Clint said. "That still doesn't excuse you for having him killed."

"I didn't! I told Red from the very beginning that I would be his woman, but that he would have to take me for what I am, not for my husband's money. And he promised he would."

"But he didn't."

Her eyes dropped to the ground and the angry fire died in her. "No," she whispered. "He abducted me on the street, knowing that Hank Tilson would come and that Simon would have no choice but to go along. For him to remain in Desert Springs would have been a public admission of cowardice. A man, even a rich and powerful one, who would not go after his own wife would become an object of scorn."

"So Red killed him."

"Maybe he would have let him live if you hadn't shown

up! I don't know. But when he died, I knew that Red was at fault and that he had deceived me and ought to hang.''

''And you were really going to testify against him in Phoenix?''

''I think I would have. Even loving him, I would have.''

Clint expelled a deep breath. ''Look,'' he said tiredly, ''why don't you just tell Mando and me where you think this Shatto took Maria. Then we can cut across to a stage station and send you on back to Desert Springs where you belong.''

''I don't belong there anymore.''

''Then go wherever you do belong!'' Clint was getting impatient. He had made love to her and she had loved Red Taggert while doing it with him. Now she said she was sorry. He had seen the loathing and disgust for Red on her face when Red admitted he had sold Maria to the Apache chief. So everything considered, he guessed he still did not quite know where the woman stood and whether she could be trusted.

''Clint,'' she told him quietly, ''I think that right now I belong with you and Mando. It is my one chance to do something good and decent. Maybe saving that girl will balance some of the harm I have done up to now.''

''Yeah, and it might get you raped and scalped,'' he said tightly. ''Have you thought of that?''

''Yes. I'm going anyway.''

''Damn!'' he cussed. ''All right, get your things together, find a horse, and saddle it. We leave within the hour.''

''Thank you,'' she said gratefully.

It was not what he had expected her to say. Clint clenched his teeth. ''Damn!'' He grunted again as he went off to reclaim his horse.

Chapter Thirty

It was amazing how a man felt a lot more like a man on a good horse. With Duke instead of a mule, Clint sat tall in the saddle and he could see the country as it needed seeing. Not that he hadn't appreciated Boris' mules, because he sure had, but no mule could run like Duke or carry him so far and so fast.

Duke seemed plenty glad to be reunited, too. Maybe he was expecting Clint to ride him the hell out of the desert, back up to Wyoming or Colorado, any damn place where there was grass instead of cactus, rock, and sand. If that were the case, Clint knew he was going to have to disappoint the big black gelding because Shatto was not going north, but dead south toward Mexico.

Both Clint and Mando were handsome men, men who could usually have their way with even the stubbornest woman, but they had met their match in Jane Gottman. They had tried everything to get her to tell them where Shatto had gone, or at least where she thought he intended to go, but Jane refused to talk.

It was frustrating to both men and it wounded their pride just a little. Jane seemed to understand their game and she realized that, once she told them where the Apache chieftain was headed, they would leave her and go on alone. The woman had set it into her mind that she had to redeem herself by somehow putting her life in danger in an attempt to save Maria.

So they rode south day after day, seeing nothing but the

heat riding hell over the land. The sun was brutal and un-relenting and even Duke seemed oppressed. His head hung low as he walked.

They splashed across the Gila River after filling their canteens. None of them wanted to go any further south, for they knew that the deeper they went, the greater the danger from the Apache. Yuma lay somewhere to the west and a hell of a lot farther to the east lay Tucson, but to the south there was just more desert and death and Mexico.

For days they rode and then they were in the Great Desert and south of the border. The country changed not a bit at the border, but Mando pinpointed the crossing and swore that the country changed for the better; this made Clint smile.

Mando removed his hat and wiped his brow of sweat. He looked at Jane with a cocked eye. "Well, señora, how much farther south do we go? Fairly soon we will be up to our asses in the Gulf of Mexico."

"South," she said. "We can't stop now."

Mando scowled. "Soon we will have to stop."

Jane gave no answer but kept riding.

That night, the woman seemed restless. They had covered a long, hard trail through brutal country and she should have fallen asleep the moment her head touched the saddle, but she didn't. Mando was sleeping, though; his soft snoring kept the breeze moving and Clint wondered how the man survived in Apache country when he slept so noisily at night.

"Clint," she whispered.

He rolled over in his blankets to look at her. "What?"

"I have a confession to make," she said quietly.

"Jesus Christ," he groaned, not liking the sound of her voice and dreading whatever it was she was going to tell him. Not once in his entire adulthood had any woman ever given him even a hint of good news when she began by offering a confession.

"Jane, if you are going to tell me you have been leading Mando and me on a wild-goose chase and that you haven't the least idea of where that poor girl is, I think you had better just climb on your horse and hope the Apache catch you before me or Mando.''

"That bad, huh?''

''We are not down here on a vacation,'' he told her. ''This is rough, dangerous country in case you forgot, and I can feel the hair on my scalp digging in and praying not to be lifted off by some Indian. Now, what is the confession?''

''Well, it's about Shatto and where he might be.''

''Might be? You are supposed to know where he is!''

''Now, calm down, Clint. This is a big country and he is an Apache. I mean, it is not like there is a town and a street address. It's not like that at all.''

''Would you just get to the confession and stop trying to soften me up for the bad news?''

''Well, I don't know exactly where this Shatto fella is going. Fact is, I never even saw the man. You see, Red took that poor girl off and sold her; Shatto and his men would not ride into the volcano for fear that it would be a trap.''

''Then if you didn't see Shatto or even watch him ride away, how do you know where he might have gone?''

''Because I overheard someone say that Maria was going to Mexico City.''

Clint sat up fast on his blanket. ''You mean you think we'll have to ride clear—''

''No, no,'' she said quickly. ''I don't!''

''Then . . .''

''The man I overheard also said that she was going by ship—that Shatto was going to meet a ship at the head of the Gulf of Mexico.''

''Are you sure?''

''Of course I'm sure! Do you think that I would bring us all the way into this godforsaken country if I weren't sure? This time, I am telling you the truth, Clint! You have to believe me.''

He stared at the stars. ''I don't reckon I have a whole lot of choice in the matter, Jane. Besides, we'll find out when we get to the Gulf of Mexico.''

"If they are there, how are you going to save her from Shatto?"

"I don't know. We'll just play it as it goes."

"It may go very bad, Clint."

He smiled grimly. "I think you can almost count on that. Now go to sleep, Jane."

"I'm not sleepy. I was thinking that we may die tomorrow. And I was thinking that if this is my last night on earth, that it was lousy to spend it doing nothing but lying here tossing all alone."

Clint sat bolt upright. He remembered how it had been making love to Jane Gottman, and even though she wasn't as passionate or as savage as Rita had been, she was damn fine. Damn fine!

"You thinking what I think you're thinking?"

"If you mean, do I want you with me tonight, then the answer is yes."

Clint grinned broadly and moved over to her. "This could be the last night of our lives, Jane, and you are right to think it would be a shame to waste it on sleep."

She reached for him. "I am so glad we are finally seeing things eye to eye."

Chapter Thirty-One

Jane unbuttoned her blouse and Clint buried his face in the incredibly soft flesh of her breasts. He had forgotten how much he had enjoyed them before and how, when he played with her nipples, she had begun to squirm and moan with pleasure. Clint sucked on her nipples greedily; then his hand slipped down and unbuttoned the baggy pants she wore. When his fingers slid into the silken tangle between her legs, Jane bit him gently, and then she was frantically pulling her panties down all the way and reaching for his belt.

Clint let her unbuckle his pants and remove his boots. He let her slip his shorts off. Then she knelt over him, her mouth slipping wetly over his already stiff cock. She worked it up and down until he thought he was going to go crazy. Then he lifted her head and she smiled.

"What's the matter? Can't stand the pleasure?" she asked.

He did not feel like bantering with the woman. "Put it where it belongs, Jane."

She was happy to oblige him. She opened her legs, then took his cock, and eased down on him, her mouth forming a circle of pleasure as she growled a very low moan.

Clint was having difficulty keeping himself from making noise that might wake Mando. After all, if it were their last night to live, it probably was also Mando's, so he felt a little guilty leaving the man to his uneventful snoring.

Jane was humping faster and faster. Her hips started to rotate instead of just going up and down. She bit her lower lip and he could feel her lubricating his shaft. She lifted her hips

157

almost to the point where he was coming out, only to slam herself back down and bury him inside of her to the hilt. She was like a sailing ship riding a heavy sea, rising and falling.

Her face was alive with pleasure and now she seemed unable to stand it any longer. She pitched forward to lay her big tits over his face. Clint cupped them together and tasted them both at the same time. Jane raised her hands to her hair and shuddered with ecstasy.

He worked her like that, top and bottom, until neither of them could stand it a moment longer. Then he rolled her over and his lean, hard body took command. He gritted his teeth and kept driving in and out until she was moaning softly and thrashing. Clint felt her body stiffen all at once. Then her fingers bit into his buttocks. She was jerking him deeper as she climaxed with a tremendous shudder. Clint also reached his limit. He slammed his hips hard against her. His hot seed gushed to fill her to overflowing, and his mouth covered hers as he pinned her.

Clint held her for a full minute while his stiff cock pulsated and her body milked him. Then he rolled off her and gazed peacefully up at the sky. When he could breathe normally, he said, "Damn good idea you had, Jane. I should have thought of it myself."

Her finger stroked his chest. "It's a long night ahead and I could hardly stand not making any noise."

The wide awake and very annoyed Mando Santana said with more than a little asperity, "Lady, you made a hell of a lot of noise! And if you are fixing to do it again with him, you might not be able to keep me from coming over to sample some of your honey pot, too."

Jane covered her mouth and giggled. "I'm sorry! And I'm so embarrassed. I didn't realize you were awake."

Mando rolled over to stare at her. "I have been awake since the conversation started to get interesting. What kind of a man could sleep through something like that after just being reminded this could be his last night?"

Jane was quiet for a moment. Finally, she said, "Clint, would you be terribly offended if Mando and I—"

"Hell, no," he said with a grin, pulling on his pants and boots and grabbing his saddle, gun, and bedroll, "but I damn sure don't intend to sit here listening to you."

He saw Mando coming over and the man was already out of his clothes and primed for action. "You are going to like it," Clint said.

Mando laughed happily. "So will the beautiful Jane Gottman."

Clint lugged his gear a hundred feet or more away, and he could already hear Jane and Mando going at it hot and heavy. He smiled, stretched, and stared up at the heavens. Jane Gottman, he had decided, liked sex with anyone, anytime, as long as the man aimed to please. That was fine; better that, than a woman who had the appetite but grew bitter and hypocritical through neglect.

Clint laid back down and listened to a pack of coyotes serenading the moon. They sounded mournful. He guessed that they had every right to be, given the kind of hell they inhabited. He closed his eyes and thought about tomorrow and wondered whether they would find Maria. If they did, how the devil was he going to keep his promise to poor old Boris and free his daughter.

In his pocket still rested that pouch of gold dust and nuggets and maybe that would be enough to buy her freedom. But maybe Shatto would take the gold and try to kill them without giving up a damned thing and perhaps gaining himself another beautiful woman to use or to sell.

He heard Jane begin to moan and cry out with pleasure. Clint scowled and picked up his belongings and moved farther away. He now understood exactly what Mando had meant about finding sleep impossible when a woman was making those kinds of pleasuring noises. Better, he thought, to listen to the coyotes howl.

Chapter Thirty-Two

For obvious reasons, they slept a little late the next morning. All three smiled a little sheepishly as they broke camp. Jane Gottman looked worn out, but her head was high and she seemed to be ready to meet whatever lay ahead. And Mando was whistling a tune as he saddled her horse and helped her mount up.

"Well," Clint said, "I guess this is the day we find out whether we've been riding all these miles for nothing."

"And,": Mando added, "whether this Shatto is as dangerous as I have heard been told. The man has a reputation for double-crossing people. I do not think that he can be trusted."

"Who said anything about trust?" Clint asked. "What I have in mind is a simple purchase: the pouch of gold that Boris gave me for Maria. Don't figure it matters to Shatto who buys the girl."

"Maybe, maybe not. Shatto has nothing to lose and everything to gain by killing us and taking the señora, our horses, and weapons."

Jane rode between them. "We can talk all day, but it won't do a damned thing unless we find the man. So why don't we stop talking and just ride?"

Mando and Clint exchanged amused glances and Clint said, "We both did our share of riding last night, Jane. Could be we are a little sore in the saddle this morning."

161

She burst out laughing. They rode out of the camp then, all three of them feeling good.

The land they crossed those last few miles down to the Gulf of Mexico was barren and covered with sand dunes. The air was still and hot; they saw a few gulls in the sky, but it was not until they topped a rise and gazed down at the water itself that they really believed it was there.

"Look at that," Clint said in wonder. "Right next to the desert, a sea. Damned hard to believe."

"And look! A ship is coming!" Jane pointed to the south, and coming into view was a ship. She was running up the gulf at half-mast.

"That must be her." Clint shaded his eyes. "Damned if I can see any Indians waiting down there."

"They will be there," Mando said. "Have you thought of what we are going to do with all the other prisoners, or are we just going to let them be taken down to Mexico?"

Clint blinked. "Other prisoners? What others?"

"There will be more, I guarantee you, Gunsmith. You do not think that this ship comes all the way up here for one slave, do you?"

"Damn!" Clint swore, "I've been so busy thinking about the girl that it never occurred to me that there'd be others. But you are right, Mando. There will be others."

Mando shrugged. "I care only for the prospector's daughter and the gold she can lead us to. I will take the gold to Mexico City and use it to free my father."

Jane said, "But we can't let innocent people be sold into slavery."

"I'm not going to die and let my father rot in prison," Mando argued stubbornly, looking at Clint and waiting to hear his thoughts.

The Gunsmith counted the bullets in his cartridge belt. "Twelve," he said out loud. "Twelve and the six I have in my gun make eighteen. If there are more than eighteen warriors, then I may need some help, Mando. But if not, then you can do whatever you damn well please because any captive who wants to be freed, will get freed. Comprendes?''

"Ha!" Mando barked a laugh. "You are crazy! You would attack Shatto and his men by yourself!"

Clint just shrugged. He touched spurs to Duke's flanks and started down the towering sand dune toward the shore. He would ride along the shell-strewn beach until he came upon Shatto and his men. Then he would count them and see what would happen. Maybe the pouch of gold would be enough to settle the matter peaceably, but if not, he had not been bluffing a moment before.

Mando and Jane could do as they wanted, but he was going to do what he had set out to do and that was to save the girl and anyone else who wanted his freedom. And if this Shatto were treacherous, perhaps he would kill him quickly and his warriors would give up the fight. That was probably unrealistic because Apaches were not known to be easily dissuaded once they had a mind to do something.

To hell with it, Clint thought as Duke's hooves crunched across the shells and the ship drew ever closer. Like everything else in my lifetime, I will just play this out one step at a time.

Chapter Thirty-Three

The ship was still several miles to the south when it lowered its sails and dropped anchor. Clint watched a boat as it was lowered over the side. Then he saw a number of men climb down netting, settle into the boat, and begin to row toward shore.

He had still not seen the Apaches but that was not surprising. Clint had no doubt the Apache were just ahead, and now he drew in his horse. He asked, "Why don't we wait a few minutes and see what is going to happen next?"

"That sounds like a fine idea," Jane said. "That way, we can wait until the Apaches bring their captives down to the boat and see how many there are."

But Mando was not so agreeable. "What does it matter?" he demanded with impatience. "We probably haven't enough gold to buy the girl, let alone others who are with her."

"Look!" Clint cried, suddenly coming off his horse, pulling Duke behind a sand dune and out of sight, and motioning Jane and Mando to do the same quickly. "I count four women and three little girls."

"So do I," Jane said grimly. "But how many Apache?"

"Can't tell yet. Most of them are still down behind the dunes waiting."

Jane looked at him. "What are we going to do?"

"Yeah," Mando added, "that is a good question. What are we going to do?"

"I . . ." Clint closed his mouth and his spirits tumbled to

165

his feet because, suddenly, the Apaches were all filing down to the water to greet the men in the rowboat. There were no fewer than thirty of them and every one was heavily armed.

Mando glanced sideways at him and muttered, "All right, Gunsmith, what do you think we ought to do now?"

He scowled and then rested on the sand dune to think about it. Attacking thirty armed Apache would be suicidal and would accomplish nothing except getting themselves slaughtered.

"Well?" asked Mando.

Clint pulled his Stetson down low over his eyes.

"You and Jane keep a lookout and let me know if anything happens. I need to think about this awhile."

"Think?" The way Mando said it pretty well expressed his disgust with the matter. "What is there to think about, Gunsmith? We have lost this game."

"Maybe, maybe not. There is more than one way to skin a cat. If we can't attack the Indians, then we may just have to attack that Mexican ship."

Mando groaned, cussed a blue streak in Spanish, then flopped down in the hot sand, and joined Jane in watching the landing party.

Clint's eyes were closed, but his mind was churning over the idea of rescuing the woman and children from the ship. One thing for certain, the ship could not have a crew of thirty men and the crew it had could not be half as dangerous as a band of renegade Apache. It had to be easier.

"Clint! Wake up!" Mando said with excitement. "They are shaking hands now and loading the women and children on the boat. One of the Apaches is going with them!"

Clint sat up and then swiveled to gaze down the seashore toward the landing party and the Apache warriors. It all looked so friendly and peaceable—the way the Indians were waving and the sailors were waving back as they rowed the slaves to the ship—that it was hard to believe what was actually going on. Innocent people were being bought and sold, exiled, never to see their homeland or their loved ones again.

"We can't just sit here and watch!" Jane cried, starting to come to her feet and run for her horse.

Clint just managed to grab her by the ankle and pull her down. She struggled hard until he said, "There is nothing we can do until tonight!"

"Tonight, what makes you think they will be there tonight?" She stared up at him in fury.

"Because Mando said one of the Apaches was going onboard. That will be Shatto. Isn't that right, Mando?"

The young man nodded. "That's true, but—"

"And Shatto," Clint continued, "will be taken to the captain's quarters and feted. Probably given liquor to drink and rich food. Maybe also given a few weapons and trinkets. They will make that Apache chief look special in the eyes of his tribesmen. He is being honored and the ship will not leave until the morning when the wind and the tide are favorable."

"How do you know all this?"

"Just a guess," Clint admitted. "But if you were the captain, would you be stupid enough to go ashore and risk being taken hostage by an Apache known to be a double-crosser? Of course not! Why take the risk? So you would have one of your men do the bargaining so that you seemed above it all. And then, because you profit from Shatto and his slaves, you know you must honor him, make him look special so that he will steal more hostages and come again to deal soon."

Mando stared at him. "You are a pretty smart hombre."

Clint grinned modestly. "I have dealt with Indians before. Face is everything. Shatto would lose face if he did not powwow with the captain of that vessel himself and only a fool of a captain would take the risk of going ashore. The rest seemed easy enough to figure out."

"All right," Jane said. "So that is Shatto being rowed to the ship. What do we do now?"

"Simple," Clint said, "if you both know how to swim, we visit the ship tonight and set things right."

"I can't swim!" Mando swore. "Not a lick!"

"I can swim," Jane said, "but not that far."

Clint scowled, aware that they were staring at him, waiting for his reaction. He lay back down on the sand and again pulled his hat low over his eyes. "You both sure have a way of fouling up a fella's plans," he grumbled. "Looks like I will just have to think of something else."

"We aren't going to hold our breath," Jane said. "I can't see a way to do it."

Clint tipped his hat back for a moment to regard her thoughtfully. "There has to be a way," he told her. "And I am going to think of it before tonight."

She kissed him on the lips. "That's for luck and for . . . well, last night—not being mad or jealous about Mando. You know."

"I don't know the word jealousy," he told her. "And we aren't bound to fidelity. It was nice, Jane. And if I didn't have this rescue thing on my mind, I would like to do it all over again starting at sunset."

She grinned and teased him by saying, "You figure out a way to save those poor women from being shipped and you may have a lot more than you can rightly handle!"

"That will be the day," he laughed. "Now, please watch them and wake me up when it is about to get dark. We may have a long night ahead of us."

Chapter Thirty-Four

"Wake up, Gunsmith; it's getting dark," Jane said.

Clint opened his eyes, crawled to the the rim of the dune, and peered down the beach. The sun was getting low on the horizon and it was time to act. "Where is that rowboat?"

"Tied to the ship for the moment, though it has come back twice bringing whiskey and trade goods. All of the captives are on now and there is a hell of a wild party going on just up from the beach. The Apache are roasting a horse and celebrating with the whiskey," Mando said.

"Good," Clint said emphatically. "That is the best news I have heard in weeks. As soon as the sun vanishes, we are going to go have a closer look at the party."

"If we get too close, we might end up alongside the roasting horse," Mando warned, trying to make a joke but not succeeding.

Clint studied the ship intently. "Did you see where they took the women and little girls?"

"Up this right side and then down a hole that is toward the front of the ship," Mando answered.

Clint nodded. "We leave the horses here and go ahead on foot."

"Then what?" Mando asked.

"Before morning, we take a short ride," he said, moving into dusk.

They had no trouble at all approaching the drunken, feasting Apache. Clint had no intention of attacking the Apache.

He instructed Jane and Mando to dig themselves a couple of low trenches in the wet sand. Then he removed his boots and waded into the gulf. It felt like bath water. There were no waves and the stars overhead were bright. He could see by the huge fire that the Apaches were having themselves a hell of a party.

The roast horse would have smelled like beef had the Indians bothered to scrape all the hair off. Burnt hair did nothing for a man's appetite. Clint waded up to his neck and knew that, in the dark water, he was all but invisible from either the ship or the shore. He could see the Apaches dancing around the fire, eating and drinking, shoving each other playfully, and having about the same kind of fun that a crew of cowboys might have if they had food and whiskey and nothing but the sky and the land to witness whatever the hell they felt like creating.

He turned toward the ship. It was in his mind to swim out to it perhaps and climb on. Only trouble was, how could he get the captives safely ashore without Jane and Mando's help? The answer was that he could not. And what if he could get them to shore without being seen, then what? There was still a hell of a lot of desert between here and help.

Standing in the water with those kinds of problems bedeviling him, Clint wondered if he wasn't loco for even trying to save these captives. The odds against pulling off an escape seemed impossible and yet . . . yet he created his own legend by taking on impossible odds and making them work in his favor. The Gunsmith was known far and wide as a man who never tallied up the odds, as one who just went ahead with what was the right thing to do and to the devil with the odds.

Clint stood in the water until his skin puckered. Back on shore the Apache fell silent, passed out on the whiskey or asleep, it did not matter. He was having a difficult time staying awake until a large, spiny fish brushed his ankle. Then he was wide awake and praying it was no shark or something looking for food. Later, he guessed it was about two in the morning, he heard laughter from the Mexican ship and saw the silhouettes of four men emerge on the deck.

He wished he had his gun, but he knew that the water would foul the mechanism, so he had left it on shore and taken a knife as his only weapon. The laughter carried across the water and Clint could tell by their voices that they were pretty drunk. He waited until he heard the Spanish word *adiós*, and then he knew the waiting was almost over.

This was confirmed a few minutes later when he identified the dark form of Shatto because of a feather in his hair; the Apache chief was accompanied by a trio of sailors. All of them descended the webbed ropes and plopped into the boat, almost capsizing it and finding that hilariously funny. A moment later, the splash of oars told Clint the boat was coming his way. He had hoped that there would be only two sailors, but now he saw that two were needed to row and a third would be steering the tiller. Clint turned to study the exact spot on the beach where the boat would most likely touch land. This was where Mando and Jane waited in their wet, shallow trench and where thousands of hungry little sand crabs had probably been biting the hell out of them for hours. Oars began to dip steadily as the boat moved swiftly to shore.

Clint turned to see it coming and he ducked his head under and swam through the inky water toward shore. When he reached shallows, he flattened out and waited, staying under the surface as much as he could. The boat was right behind him. When he heard its bow scrape the sand, Clint slipped completely under the water and moved quickly. He was not ten feet away from the boat. When his hands touched the wooden hull, he planted his feet into the sand and heaved upward with all of his might, praying his timing was correct.

The boat was big and heavy and he did not try to lift it completely out of the water but only to make it lurch heavily to one side. He knew the moment that four bodies crashed into the water that he had succeeded. Clint lunged at them and his knife buried itself deep into Shatto's heart. He pulled it free and went for a sailor who came up spluttering. Mando was flying across the shallow water and lunging with his own knife. Before anyone could cry out in alarm, the Mexicans were dragged underwater and killed.

Without speaking, Jane joined them. They quickly changed into the sailors' uniforms and got the rowboat turned back out toward the ship. ''You steer, Jane. Mando and I will do our best at rowing to the ship.''

She nodded, her face pale in the moonlight. Possibly she was shocked by the swift finality of Clint and Mando's attack moments before and the floating bodies already bobbing in the water. Clint did not have time to worry about that now. Shatto had died in battle and that was important to a warrior.

Clint knew that rescuing the captives was still almost impossible. If anything, Shatto's death and the certain discovery of his floating body in the morning would cause the Apaches to go wild with a need for revenge.

Clint pulled his oar very hard, too hard, for the boat momentarily swerved off its course until he eased up and matched Mando's strength and stroke.

As they neared the ship, it seemed they were looking up at an entire mountain range. The deck above them appeared incredibly high. Clint stopped pulling on the oar and let the boat glide the last few yards until it quietly thumped up against the netting. They lifted the oars and laid them inside. Clint found a rope and securely tied the boat to the rope webbing. He had not forgotten that neither Jane nor Mando was capable of swimming. They had to have the boat to escape with the captives—but first, they had to find them and return without being seen or heard.

Clint took a deep breath and grabbed hold of the ropes. He stuck his bare foot into one of the big squares and placed his weight on it. The rope collapsed in on his ankle and the whole thing swayed wildly.

Clint did not dare look back at Jane or Mando or let them see that getting up to the swaying deck, which seemed so far overhead, was going to be damned difficult. So he did the only thing he could do and that was grab hold firmly and start climbing, hoping and praying that there was not some Mexican sentry waiting topside for the return of the three sailors.

But even if there were, Clint figured that, dressed in uniform and with the knife clenched tightly between his teeth, he still had a fighting chance if he could reach the deck. And that was all the Gunsmith had ever needed.

Just a fighting chance.

Chapter Thirty-Five

Clint made it up to the deck a lot more quickly than he had expected. There was a knack to climbing that rope web and it did not take long to figure it out. Now, if there had been a rough sea, things might have been different, but the water was as smooth as a billiard ball. That was going to make getting the women and children down to the rowboat a whole lot easier.

He gave Jane a hand up and Mando came right behind. As soon as he was on deck, he pointed down the starboard side of the ship where he saw a hatch. In silence, he led the way. When he reached the hatch, he knelt and studied the entire deck. There was probably a sentry somewhere, but it was also likely the man was asleep, for there was no apparent danger.

Clint grabbed the hatch cover and gave it a good yank. It came off in his hands, and he placed it on the deck. He motioned Jane to kneel forward, peer down into the pitch black, and then to speak softly to the captives. They had already talked this over, and it was decided that a woman's voice was a lot less likely to raise a cry of alarm than either his own or Mando's.

"Hello," Jane whispered, "hello, down there. I came to help you. I am an American who—"

A hand came out of the darkness and it did not belong to a woman or a child. It was powerful. It grabbed Jane and yanked her down into the hold.

For an instant, even Clint was stunned by the sudden unexpectedness of the hand. But then he heard Jane's body slam into the floor of the hold. It was followed by her muffled cry for help.

"Stay here!" Clint hissed as he leaped into the hold and fell ten feet to land on a Mexican sailor who had Jane by the throat and was throttling the life out of her.

There was a single candle burning in the hold. In one swiftly passing instant during his fall, Clint had the image of a crowd of huddled woman and children packed together at one end of the stinking hold. Then he was fighting for his life and that of Jane.

The sailor was big and strong. Clint was lunging for the man, and his fist connected and sent the sailor slamming against the bulkhead.

A little girl opened her mouth to scream and her mother clamped a hand over her mouth. The Mexican raised his head to cry out for help. Clint's fist slammed into his jaw and he dropped like a rock; he would be out for a long time.

"Are you all right?" Jane asked in a strangled voice.

He looked up at her. "Yeah. Why don't you tell these folks who we are and what we came for. Tell them the chances of us all getting killed are better than average. A lot better. There are no guarantees, only. . . ."

"For a man of action," a stout, middle-aged woman said as she knelt by the unconscious sailor and stuffed a rag in his mouth, "you sure do talk plenty, Gunsmith. We don't want or expect any guarantees, just a chance to go home alive." She then began to bind the guard's hands and feet with strips torn from her dress.

He grinned. "We aim to do our best, ma'am. But it's a mighty long way from here to anyplace."

"I can shoot a gun straight. So can a couple of the other women. What do you want us to do?" she asked, finishing with the sailor and coming to stand before him with her hands on her broad hips.

"Climb the ladder and follow us off this boat," he told

her. "We'll row to shore and take it from there."

"We are going to walk the desert?"

Clint shook his head. "I just haven't thought that far, ma'am. All I know is that we haven't got time to discuss it right here and now."

The woman was obviously the leader of the pitiful little collection and now she turned to face the others. "Is there anybody afraid to go and who wants to stay here and wind up deep in the guts of Mexico, the slave of some rich patron?"

They all shook their heads vigorously, especially a pretty young woman in the back who Clint thought might be Boris' daughter. "Then let's get off this tub! Girls first; then ladies, you go right after them."

The Gunsmith was already on his way back up. When trouble came, if it came, it would be from topside now. And while he had every confidence in Mando Santana, Clint still wanted to be on top.

The clean air was like a tonic to the women and children. As soon as they felt it, they seemed to come alive. The sluggishness of their movements vanished and now they were stepping lively as they were led to the rope webbing and told to climb down to the boat tied below. To demonstrate how easy it was, Jane went first. After that, the girls did it as if it were the most natural thing in the world to dangle on rope twenty or thirty feet above the water.

Clint and Mando stayed until the captives were all seated in the boat.

"You go ahead," Clint said.

"What about you?"

"I'll be along in a few minutes. Maybe Jane can use the other oar and someone else can steer. I just want to make sure that no one sees the boat leaving and opens fire. You would be like sitting ducks out on that moonlit water. I can't take the chance."

Mando nodded with reluctance. "You come quickly, Gunsmith. We've got to figure out how to get out of this place damned quick."

"You know that there is only one answer to that," Clint said. "We have to play Indian and steal horses and run those we don't need off into the dunes—then ride like hell."

"Yeah," Mando said, "I know. But look at those women and children; they're weak and some of them look pretty bad."

"You figure out yet which one is Maria?"

Mando shook his head. "It's dark and I was trying to help the girls and. . . ."

Clint patted his shoulder. "If you don't be careful, I'm going to think you have a heart after all, Mando. Go ahead now."

He nodded. "Once we get out of gun range, you dive and swim, Gunsmith. There isn't any of us who will make it without you."

"Sure you would," he answered. "Now, get out of here."

Clint watched them leave and then he started moving down the side of the ship. He knew that there was a sentry aboard and that the man might awaken and sound the alarm. If he did, not only would the boat bulging with captives be at their mercy, but the firing would also alert the sleeping Apaches.

Either way spelled disaster. Clint was going to make damn sure the decks were swept clean.

Chapter Thirty-Six

Time was running out. Clint had gone clear up to the bow of the Mexican ship and had seen nothing. Now he was stalking along the port side. Suddenly he saw a movement in the shadows and then a sleepy voice drawled something in Spanish.

"Sí," Clint said, moving forward like a cat. Too late the sentry realized that the Gunsmith was not one of the crew. The Mexican sailor's mouth opened to shout a startled warning and Clint filled it with his knuckles.

The man staggered and groped for his knife. Clint struck him with a thundering left uppercut. The sentry went down hard and Clint moved on quickly.

When he had reached the stern of the ship, he climbed up on the gunnel, grabbed a rope to steady himself, and peered down at the water far below and then out to where the overburdened boat was doggedly making its way to the shore. It was almost ready to beach, and so far there had been no alarm sounded. Clint studied the dark waters with real trepidation. As a little kid, he had once dived off a cliff into a river. It had been no higher than this. He had done it to escape an enraged mother bear whose cub he had taken an unhealthy delight in chasing.

Clint swallowed. God it was a long way down! He took a deep breath, closed his eyes, and jumped.

It seemed to take forever for his body to smash into the water. The impact was much harder than he thought it would be, and for a brief instant he was stunned and felt himself struggling as he sank. It was a horrifying experience, knowing you were sinking and not being able to command your arms and legs to work and drive you back up to breathe. Clint sank to a depth of twenty feet and then he began to rise—slowly at first, and then faster as he stroked feebly. His lungs were bursting. Clint expelled the dead air and gulped in fresh at the very instant his head broke the water's surface.

He found his bearings and then he began to swim toward shore with powerful strokes. Behind him, the ship lay silent and forbidding, and before him, he could now see the women and children being unloaded and hurried northward along the beach.

As Clint waded to shore, Mando caught his arm and helped him stand. Clint was winded, his limbs felt leaden after the long swim, and he had to lean on Mando a little until he was standing firmly on dry land. "Where is Jane?" he asked breathlessly.

"We decided that she should stay with the children, some of whom are not strong enough to go very far without help."

Clint wearily raised his head and remembered Maria as he stared at a beautiful, young woman in front of him.

She stepped forward to take his hand and peer at the turquoise ring he wore. "I have to know why you are wearing my father's wedding ring. If you killed him, I will—"

"No," Mando hissed. "This is the Gunsmith! He promised your father that he would come and save you from Red Taggert."

At the mention of the outlaw's name, Maria spat. "I hate him. He lied to me and then sold me to Shatto. I wish him dead!"

"Your wish has come true," Clint said. "I killed him. Here," he added as he reached into his pocket and pulled out the pouch of gold. "A gift from your father."

"Keep it," she told him. "What good is gold in a place like this? We must steal horses and hurry away!"

"That's right," Clint said. "So why don't you—"

"Go with the women?" Maria shook her head fiercely.

"You forget I am part Apache. I will steal the horses for you. If either of you tried, you would surely fail. We would all be caught and suffer worse than you can imagine."

Mando and Clint exchanged glances. "I think we had better let her lead this raid," Clint said. "She may be right."

"She is a girl!"

"I am a woman and the only chance any of us has!" Maria said in a low, hard whisper. "Is this macho of yours, this foolish pride, worth all of our lives!"

Clint shook his head. He walked to the dune and picked up his gun, holster, and cartridge belt.

Mando did not like relying on a woman to save his skin, but he had to admit that stealing horses was not one of his greatest skills. "All right. You lead and we will follow."

"Good," she said. "You must both stay back and let me go in among the horses and bring them out to you."

"Why?"

"Because you are white," Maria said simply. "I have been with the Apache long and am like them."

The explanation made a lot of sense, so they followed Maria who skirted the camp. Having been with the Apache, she knew the horses, knew also that they would be tethered to rope. She also indicated that there would be no guards, not tonight, after such a celebration and with no thought of danger.

They halted just outside the string of horses and Clint guessed there were at least thirty, all of them nothing but skin and bones. Some, however, must have been a lot stronger than the others because Maria was very deliberate in her choice of mounts. When she had untied seven, she brought them to Clint and Mando who waited at a respectful distance.

They mounted the small ponies without any difficulty using pieces of rope and crude reins Maria had also taken. Riding three, they led the others away. In the sand the hooves did no more than whisper faintly.

"You did it, Maria!" Mando said, his voice low with excitement. "You were magnificent!"

The girl was tall and lithe; her black hair hung to her slender waist. When she turned to look at Mando, her high cheeks were etched sharply against the pale moon. "Of course," she said with amusement. "Do you think I would say I could do something that I could not?"

"No, but—"

"It is to the credit of both of you that you did not let pride stand in the way of good sense."

"And that," Clint said dryly to Mando, "is about as close to a compliment as either of us is going to get from her."

"I think you are right, Gunsmith. This girl is filled with too much pride of her own."

"And you!" The girl's eyes stormed with anger at Mando. "You strut like a young peacock!"

"Enough!" Clint said roughly. "You can argue later. We have women and children to help, and this time, Mando, you and I have a man's job to do."

"Scatter the remaining Indian horses?"

"Yes," Clint said. "If we fail to do that, they will easily overtake and kill us."

"That is a man's work," Mando said with satisfaction as he glared at the girl with a look of superiority.

"I can shoot and ride as well as you, Peacock," Maria said scornfully. "Let me come, too."

"No," Clint said in a tone that brooked no argument. "This time, you are needed to help Jane and the women and children ride away as fast as they can."

Maria opened her mouth to protest, but the determined look on Clint's face seemed to tell her that the decision was final. To her credit, the girl slipped off her own pony, began to help Jane calm the children, and then place them on the backs of the smallest ponies. One of the women began to cry softly that she did not know how to ride without a saddle, but Jane and Maria convinced her that that there was never going to be a better time to learn than now.

Jane came up to Clint as he mounted Duke. "Be careful," she said quietly. "I don't want anything to happen to you."

He reached down and touched her face. "Ride back over our tracks straight north and do not stop if you hear gunfire. Just keep going as fast as you can. Promise?"

She nodded. A child began to whimper and she moved away to help.

"Let's go," Clint said.

Mando nodded. He and Maria were staring at each other across a distance of less than twenty feet. Maria was holding a child on an pony, calming the babe but all the time studying Mando.

"Vaya con Dios, Peacock," she said softly.

Mando should have gotten angry, but there was something in the tone of the girl's voice that pulled him up short and then made him sit taller in the saddle. He tipped his hat to Maria and smiled before he spun his horse and followed Clint back toward the Apache camp.

Chapter Thirty-Seven

Like an invisible paint brush, dawn was streaking color across the sky. Clint and Mando drove into the Apache camp and slashed the tether rope with their knives and scattered the Indian ponies.

Normally, the Apache would have been awake by then, Shatto would have shouted battle orders, and the likelihood was that Clint and Mando would have been ripped out of their saddles in a volley of gunfire. But the Apaches had hangovers and were unusually slow to respond and Shatto was floating dead somewhere out in the Gulf of Mexico.

Clint and Mando opened fire. They each grabbed a goatskin filled with gallons of precious water. The Apaches finally staggered to their feet in confusion and chaos. A few warriors, perhaps those with clearer heads, began to snatch their weapons and return fire.

Clint reined Duke in behind a sand dune and shouted, "Mando, chase those ponies as far as you can and then join the others!"

Mando knew better than to waste time in arguing, for he understood that the thin, weakened ponies would not run far unless driven.

Clint got down from Duke, scrambled up to the crest of a dune, and opened fire on the advancing Apaches. He dropped two with two shots and the others momentarily disappeared. They were going to try to circle behind him and then close the trap. Clint saw a head move and he snapped off a shot, knowing that he had missed. He could hear Mando's shouts at the Indian ponies growing dimmer as he drove them farther and farther away.

The Apaches were desperate to kill him and retrieve their horses. Clint could feel them coming around behind him, so he waited until one more showed his face. Then he dropped the man, took a moment to reload, and decided he had pushed his luck to the very limit. He mounted his horse.

Duke also felt the trap closing around them. He charged, running as hard as he could through the loose sand. Apaches seemed to sprout from the sandy earth before them, and Clint's gun met them with lead and death while Duke never veered from his chosen path of escape. Two more Apaches went down. A third jumped at Clint and was knocked spinning by Duke's powerful shoulder. Then, they were scrambling over the crest of another dune, and Duke finally seemed to achieve solid footing. His speed now came into play. With bullets flying, the Gunsmith bent low in the saddle beside the goatskin waterbag and swept on. He finally overtook Mando. They pushed themselves without mercy until they overtook the women and children.

Jane and Maria fell back slightly. There was a questioning look on their faces that vanished when they saw Clint and Mando.

Clint twisted around in his saddle. He could see the Apaches on the crest of a sandy, windswept hill, and they were raising hell, but their voices were swept away by a breeze. Farther on, Clint could see the top half of the main mast of the Mexican ship. He turned back around in his saddle. "How are the children doing?" he asked Jane.

"Fine," she said, "all of them are going to make it."

"You bet they are," Clint said with a tired grin as he proudly watched the bedraggled band of captives they had rescued from a lifetime of bondage.

"Are you all right?"

"Never felt better," he answered.

Jane looked at Mando and Maria who were riding side by side. "Is she, you know, is she going to find her father's gold so that he can free his own father from the Mexican authorities?''

"I don't know," Clint said with a shrug of his shoulders as he glanced sideways at the pair. "But from what I have seen so far, I believe Mando has finally met his match in a woman. I think she has told him without words that she has chosen him for her man."

"And how does he feel?"

Just at that moment, Mando reached out and took the beautiful girl's hand in his own and kissed it with a blend of passion and tenderness.

Clint laughed softly. "I think he feels the same way as Maria."

"And what about us?" Jane asked. "I am now a very wealthy widow with a lot of money."

Clint glanced up at the fiery sun. It was going to be another blistering day in this desert hell, and there would be many more of them before they crossed the border and reached the comforts of civilization. But when they did, he guessed he would let this woman treat him to a good steak dinner and a bottle of champagne. Until then, they could just keep pretending that every night they were together was going to be their last on this earth.